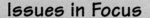

Issues in Focus

The Internet
Surfing the Issues

Anita Louise McCormick

Enslow Publishers, Inc.

40 Industrial Road   PO Box 38
Box 398   Aldershot
Berkeley Heights, NJ 07922   Hants GU12 6BP
USA   UK
http://www.enslow.com

Library of Congress Cataloging-in-Publication Data

McCormick, Anita Louise.
   The Internet : surfing the issues / Anita Louise McCormick.
      p.   cm. — (Issues in focus)
   Includes bibliographical references and index.
   Summary: Discusses the development of the Internet as a worldwide communications network, examining the possibilities and problems presented by this advance in technology.
   ISBN 0-89490-956-8
   1. Internet (Computer network)—Juvenile literature. [1. Internet (Computer network)] I. Title. II. Series: Issues in focus (Springfield, N.J.)
   TK5105.875.I57M3815   1998
   004.67'8—dc21   98-12673
                                                         CIP
                                                         AC

Printed in the United States of America

10 9 8 7 6 5 4 3

Illustration Credits: Blacksburg Electronic Village, <http://www.bev.net>, p. 87; Rachelle Chong, p. 55; Computer Virus Myths home page, p. 75; Courtesy of the Federal Bureau of Investigation, p. 45; Anita Louise McCormick, pp. 82, 93, 96, 105, 108; © 1997 Monorail Inc. All rights reserved. Monorail is a trademark of Monorail Inc., p. 84; Courtesy of National Oceanic and Atmospheric Administration, p. 14; Net Nanny, Ltd., p. 59; Daryl Popkes, p. 30; Toshiba Infinia 7231, p. 33; Courtesy of U.S. Department of Education, p. 28; Courtesy of U.S. Library of Congress, p. 11; Bastian Van Elderen, *Executive*, The Scriptorium: Center for Christian Antiquities, p. 7; WebTV and WebTV Network are trademarks of WebTV Networks, Inc., p. 83; Allan H. Weiner, p. 16.

Cover Illustration: © Corel Corporation.

Contents

1 The Exciting World
of the Internet 5

2 How the Internet Is
Changing Our Lives 24

3 Who Controls the Internet? . . . 40

4 Security on the Internet 63

5 Who Uses the Internet? 80

6 How Large Can the
Internet Grow? 90

7 The Future of the Internet 102

Guide to Internet
Newsgroups 110

Organizations to Contact 112

The Development
of the Internet 115

Chapter Notes 117

Glossary 123

Further Reading 125

Index 127

1

The Exciting World of the Internet

Students from Zeeland Middle School in Grand Haven, Michigan, were puzzling over the fragments of an ancient clay vase. As they studied the shapes and sizes of the pieces, they gradually saw how the fragments fit together. Finally, the last jagged piece was fastened into place. At last, these junior archaeologists had completed their mission.

Six thousand miles away, archaeologists working on an Egyptian dig looked over the E-mail they had received from the students. The students wanted to know how things were progressing with the

5

excavation at Wadi Natrun in Egypt, where the team of archaeologists was unearthing a fourth-century Coptic monastery. [The Coptic Church is the largest Christian sect in Egypt.]

This week, the archaeologists had something very interesting to report to the students. During the preceding Saturday, the team had discovered a system of hidden chambers beneath the monastery. What were these underground chambers used for? What interesting artifacts would they contain? Would they help twentieth-century archaeologists better understand how people at the monastery lived fifteen hundred years earlier? As the archaeologists found out, so did the students.

Steven Boggess, the co-developer of "Odyssey in Egypt," an experimental program to teach young people about archeology, says, "Sometimes the only thing that students have to go on is the Indiana Jones idea. We wanted to show the real work—and joy—of taking part in a dig."[1]

The project, sponsored by the Scriptorium: Center for Christian Antiquities, located near Grand Haven, Michigan, provided the local middle schools with a curriculum that covered Egyptian history and culture, as well as science and archaeology. Dozens of photos of the dig were posted on the Internet during the ten-week project. And fragments of ancient pottery similar to those that had recently been unearthed in Egypt were sent out to the schools for the students to study and assemble. Boggess explains, "Our goal is to provide a truly interactive

The Internet provides students opportunities to learn about the world around them and the world as far away as this archaeological site in Egypt.

classroom that allows for real-time participation in a project of exploration and discovery."[2]

Throughout the program, students from Michigan middle schools used the Internet to correspond with archaeologists, Coptic monks, and other people living near the dig. Both the students and the archaeologists who took part in the program were delighted with the results. One student remarked, "It's cool that an 11-year old can take advantage of such an awesome thing!"[3]

In the past, students wanting to learn how archaeologists work had to search for the information in textbooks and encyclopedias, or perhaps on videotapes. But a new communications tool, the Internet, has opened up new possibilities to these Michigan middle-school students—as well as to millions of other people around the world.

What Is the Internet?

It seems that no day goes by without a story involving the Internet making the news. With all that has been said about the Internet, it is easy to see why most teenagers cannot wait to explore it.

The Internet is an entirely new kind of communications medium. It is different from the thousands of radio and television stations that broadcast news, music, entertainment, and sports throughout America. It is also different from magazines, newspapers, and books. Despite all the information and entertainment that other media outlets provide, they all have one drawback. For the most part, the communication they offer is a one-way street.

Power to the People

The Internet is unique because it is interactive. In other words, it furnishes users with two-way communication. Any man, woman, teenager, or child who has access to the Internet can use it to communicate with any other Net citizen (people who are connected to the Internet) anywhere in the world.

True, broadcast stations do ask for public input from time to time. And newspapers reserve a small amount of space for "Letters to the Editor." But ultimately, the final decision about what is read, seen, and heard is up to management. The Internet is different, though, because it allows the individuals who use it to determine what is communicated through its resources. Linda J. Engelman, author of the book, *Interacting on the Internet*, said of this new medium,

> *In the past, the opportunity to deliver important missives [messages] to a worldwide audience might only be possible if you had the money, power, or fame (and often you needed all three). Thanks to the Internet, however, ordinary citizens can speak to a captive global audience. Think of the Net as a huge pulpit where every evening is 'open mic night.' As Internauts [people who use the Internet], we can stand up to the microphone and express our opinions and ideologies.*[4]

The Internet can be used to reach people in many ways. You can send E-mail (electronic messages) to anyone in the world who subscribes to an Internet service. You can post information on newsgroups, Web pages, or other Net (informal way of referring to the Internet) sites, where thousands of people are sure to see it.

A World of Information

In addition to being a great way to communicate, the Internet contains one of the most extensive collections of information ever assembled by humankind. It would take a lifetime to explore the resources the Internet holds in some categories of information.

Databases that are stored in the memories of

computers around the world are available through the Internet with the press of a few keys on a computer. Each of these computerized databases contains information that was compiled and posted by an Internet user somewhere in the world. Some databases were set up by government agencies. The Library of Congress, for example, provides Internet users with databases that contain information on nearly every book that has been published in the United States, as well as books that were published in some foreign countries.

Other databases on the Internet were set up by educational institutions, businesses, government agencies, and individuals. Some databases contain text files, and others include drawings, photographs, charts, and other graphics. They can even contain sound and video files.

For the most part, information on the Internet can be accessed in the following ways:

- E-mail—Letters and messages transmitted electronically through the Internet.

- Newsgroups—Bulletin-board-type discussion groups on the Internet.

- FTP (File Transfer Protocol)—A system that transfers files through the Internet from one computer to another.

- Telnet—A system that allows computer programs to be run by another user in a remote location.

Learn about the 1998 <u>American Memory Fellows Program</u>!
Apply for an opportunity to join teachers and media specialists in improving the teaching of American history and culture through the use of new information technologies.

Use Pathfinder indexes to guide you through American Memory historical collections and other Library of Congress resources.

<u>"Immigration in American Memory</u>," a new Feature Presentation for the <u>National History Day</u> competition!

<u>Port of Entry</u> - Use your detective skills to uncover the stories of immigrants to the United States!
The Big Picture! Weekly jigsaw puzzles with American Memory photographs.

Find <u>*Historian's Sources*</u>, a <u>*Framework for Using Primary Sources*</u>, and more!

Please take a few minutes to help us better serve your needs by completing the <u>American Memory User Survey</u>.

<u>Citing Electronic Sources</u> | <u>Comments</u> | <u>Copyright and Other Restrictions</u> | <u>Internet Resources</u> | <u>Technical Information</u>

Library of Congress URL: http://www.loc.gov/

Questions about American Memory? <u>NDLP Reference Librarian</u>: ndlpedu@loc.gov

Learning Page URL: http://lcweb2.loc.gov/ammem/ndlpedu/index.html

Jan-98

This Website, the Library of Congress Learning Page, at <http://www.lcweb2.loc.gov/ammem/ndlpedu>, provides links to a variety of educational materials and sites.

- Mailing Lists—Similar to newsgroups, only the postings are sent through E-mail to all members instead of being displayed on a bulletin board.

- IRC (Internet Relay Chat)—A system that allows Net citizens to go into Internet "chat rooms" and talk to each other.

- Gopher searches—A program that provides links to some Internet resources through a series of menus.

- The World Wide Web (WWW)—A system of connecting Internet information through Web pages and links. These pages can include text, graphics, sound files, video clips, and chat rooms.

The World Wide Web

The World Wide Web is one of the newest formats for presenting information on the Internet. Web pages can combine both text and graphics with sound files, video clips, and even 3-D images.

One unique feature of the World Wide Web is its ability to link information. Links (also known as hyperlinks) are embedded in the document and are underlined or highlighted so they can be distinguished from the rest of the text. Others may be listed for viewing at the end of the document. In either case, they give Web users the option of deciding how and when they want to access information. A link allows users to decide what path they want to follow without having to search through material they are not really interested in.

For example, if you are reading an article on a Web page about NASA's exploration of the moon, you might be able to click on the words *lunar lander* to see a photograph of the lander or learn more about it. From the lunar lander picture, you might follow links to additional pictures and text documents or to audio recordings of radio transmissions made by the first astronauts to land on the moon. Links can be written by the same person who designed the Web page. Or they can just as easily connect you to information that is posted on a Web site on the other side of the earth.

New software developments are making the Internet even more exciting. Web sites that are designed using Sun Microsystems Java software, for example, allow small programs known as Applets to be transferred to your computer. These Java Applets can contain sound, animation, graphic presentations, short videos, moving 3-D images, or any other type of program that your computer is capable of running. On-line games that were designed with Java Applets are more responsive than anything that has come before them.

A Web Site of Your Own

Today, having a Web site is not just for businesses, government agencies, and other institutions. Nearly anyone who has access to the Internet can have a Web page of his or her own. A Web page can be used

The NOAA Weather Page

NOAA Sources of Weather Information:

- NOAA Home Page including:
  - Plans for upgrading the National Weather Service
  - General information on NOAA programs and offices
- NOAA National Weather Service
  - Arkansas-Red Basin River Forecast Center
  - National Operational Hydrologic Remote Sensing Center measures snow cover in the United States and Canada
  - National Weather Service Office, Seattle, Washington
  - National Weather Service Office, Tallahassee, Florida
- NOAA Forecast Systems Laboratory (FSL)
- NOAA National Climatic Data Center
- NOAA Defense Meteorological Satellite Program (DMSP) Archive at the NOAA National Geophysical Data Center including: -- includes sample imagery on the following:
  - Nighttime Lights of the World
  - Hurricanes and Tropical Storms
- Paleoenvironmental Records of Past Climate Change
- Great Lakes Forecasting System/Ohio State University, four times a day nowcasts (water temperature, currents, etc.) for Lake Erie
- Climate Diagnostics Center's United States Interactive Climate Pages
- Tropical Prediction Center (TPC)

Many sites on the Internet have weather information derived from NOAA products. The following is a list of weather related services that could be found on the Internet. If you know of a service that we have missed, please send the URL and, if possible, a short description of the service to *help@esdim.noaa.gov*. Thanks! Of course, there are no guarantees that these services are working!

Note! Good starting points:

- Topic Guide from the USENET Frequently Asked Questions on Meteorology.
- The World-Wide Web Virtual Library: Meteorology

Many weather sites around the country provide up-to-date information on local and national weather conditions. The National Oceanic and Atmospheric Administration has compiled links to these sites on one convenient Web site, found at <http://esdim.noaa.gov/weather_page/html>.

for many different things—to express personal views, advertise a product, or to just say hello to anyone who happens to stop by. As author and Internet expert James Burke expressed in an interview with *Internet World* magazine, "Basically, the Web offers the opportunity for every individual to exercise power in a way that no information structure has ever permitted before, by providing individuals with immediate and direct access to the means to publish. . . . The Web is every person's broadcasting station, every person's information-dissemination medium."[5]

Searching the Internet

With so many resources available on the Internet, no one could possibly remember where everything is located. And with the daily changes and updates in resources that are available on the World Wide Web and other parts of the Internet, no printed directory could keep you up-to-date on the best places to look for the information you are seeking. But computer experts have solved this problem. They have designed programs, known as search engines, that can look through the Internet's vast library of resources in a matter of seconds.

Yahoo, Infoseek, AltaVista, Excite, HotBot, WebCrawler, OpenText, and Lycos are among the more common search engines. With these search engines, it is relatively easy to locate information on the Internet. To use them, you simply go to the Web page that the search engine company has set up and type in words relating to the information you are seeking. The search engine then provides you with a list of Internet sites that are likely to contain that information. Your request for information is called a *query*. The more precise your query is, the more likely the search engine is to find the type of information you want.

Amateur astronomer Allan H. Weiner uses the Internet to get updates from NASA at <http://www.nasa.gov>.

Suppose you are writing a report for science class about NASA space probes that have flown past Jupiter. You want to see what information the Internet has to offer on the subject. You could request a search of the term *Jupiter* from Yahoo's home page—<http://www.yahoo.com>. In a matter of seconds, a list of Web sites that contain information on the planet Jupiter will appear on the screen.

But as you scroll down the list, you notice that many of the sites recommended have little or no information on space probes that NASA sent to explore Jupiter. So you go back to the search bar and type in *Jupiter and space probes*. That would narrow your search considerably and make it easier to find the specific information you need for your assignment.

From there, it's up to you. You might want to visit NASA's own Web site—<http://www.nasa.gov>—to read about Jupiter and see pictures taken of the giant planet from various space probes. You might want to visit the sites that various astronomy magazines have put on the Web. After that, you could read articles about NASA's missions to Jupiter in various newspapers, magazines, and scientific journals from around the world. In fact, you could follow the World Wide Web's links on the subject for hours and go anywhere your interest took you.

One thing is certain—you would find much more information on NASA's exploration of our solar system's largest planet than you would ever need to complete your report for science class.

How the Internet Began

For almost as long as computers have existed, people have been trying to find ways to link them to share data and memory resources.

In the early years of computer science, computers functioned much more slowly than they do today. A "supercomputer" from the early 1960s was large enough to fill a room, but it couldn't begin to match the power of today's least expensive desktop computers. Even then, scientists knew that if a method could be found to enable computers to talk to each other, far more could be accomplished than with a single machine.

The Internet had its beginnings in the late 1960s. At that time, the United States government was involved in the Cold War with the Soviet Union (Russia and its satellite nations). While no actual fighting occurred between the United States and the Soviet Union, there was a great deal of tension. Both sides built up their military strength and stockpiled nuclear weapons so they would be ready to fight if a real war broke out.

Officials of the United States government were concerned that the nation's military communications would be disrupted if the Soviet Union launched a nuclear attack. So the government commissioned a team of scientists to design an attack-proof computerized network. The system they proposed would connect computers located in different parts of the country. And it would connect them in such a way that messages could be rerouted through an alternate path if one part of the system was destroyed. This system, which later developed into the Internet, was called the ARPANET (**A**dvanced **R**esearch **P**rojects **A**gency **Net**work). It connected military installations, defense contractors, and a few universities. The first links of the ARPANET were installed in 1969.

In time, researchers found out that the ARPANET was good for something besides exchanging scientific data between computers. They discovered what Internet users know today—people can use interconnected computers to "talk" to each other.

The American Public Joins the Computer Revolution

At that early date, computers were still bulky machines that were difficult for most people to operate. They were also far too expensive for the average person to afford. Nearly all computers were owned by government agencies, large businesses, scientific researchers, and universities.

However, during the late 1970s, the personal computer (PC) revolution began. Several companies, including IBM and Apple, believed a market existed for smaller computers that were easier to operate. So they set out to fill this market. The first personal computers were still too expensive for most people to afford, and they were not nearly as easy to use as computers are today. This was the beginning of a revolution in the miniaturization and affordability of computers that by the mid-1990s would bring a computer into the majority of businesses, schools, libraries—as well as nearly half of the homes in America.

In the 1980s, a number of computer enthusiasts around the world were busy developing their own small-scale version of the Internet. They set up computer bulletin boards—systems that allowed anyone with a computer and modem to view information, post messages, send E-mail, or even chat with other computer users across the system. Many bulletin-board systems were operated out of private homes. Others were operated out of educational institutions and businesses. Some bulletin boards were regional, while others were set up for people who shared a common interest in topics such as computer programming or science fiction. Many of these bulletin boards could be accessed for free; other bulletin boards charged users a small monthly fee for maintenance of the equipment. During the decade, thousands of bulletin boards sprang up across the United States.

The information and activities available through these bulletin boards were extremely limited compared with what computer users have today. Still, it was the beginning of a revolution that eventually put the power of computers into the hands of average Americans.

Alternate Networks

BITNET (Because It's Time Net) was one outgrowth of the need to communicate via computer. It was created in 1981 by Ira H. Fuchs, Vice-Chancellor of

City University of New York, and Graydon Freeman, the director of the Yale Computing Center. They set up this new network so that university professors who were unable to access ARPANET would have the opportunity to use the latest technical advances to communicate with each other and exchange information.[6] BITNET expanded quickly. By 1984, approximately one hundred organizations were connected to BITNET. And by 1989, five hundred organizations had joined.[7]

In the late 1980s, the National Science Foundation developed its own computer network—NSFNET—to connect the organization's five supercomputers. Eventually, through a system of interconnecting networks, the NSFNET made the computers and resources of the National Science Foundation available to scientists working at universities and research institutions nationwide.

The popularity of BITNET, NSFNET, and privately owned bulletin boards led to the development of on-line services such as Compuserve, Prodigy, and America Online. But unlike bulletin boards, which were operated primarily by computer hobbyists, on-line services were commercial businesses. Most charged an hourly fee for access to their databases and electronic mail service. But on-line services had the advantage of being able to offer much more to their customers than the average bulletin-board system. They supplied a larger variety of databases, discussion forums, games, and other features that appealed to the computer-using public. Even though these new on-line services charged up to several dollars per hour, many computer users thought that access to the information they provided was well worth the price.

Things You Can Do on the Internet

There is no end to the things you can do on the Internet. Browsing the Web and chatting with other Net citizens in Internet chat rooms are among the most popular with the average computer user. Downloading pictures of a favorite TV star or music group can also be fun.

Although many people view the Internet as a fun place to spend a few hours of free time, it also has a more serious side. Doctors can check into the Internet to find a treatment for a rare disease. School teachers log on to the Internet to locate ideas and resources to make lessons more interesting. Astronomers from around the world use the Internet to discuss the latest findings about possible signs of life in other parts of the galaxy. And authors of fiction and nonfiction alike use the Internet to research the articles and books they write.

On the Internet, you can transmit E-mail to people around the world as easily as to a friend across town. You can read newsgroups that have been set up for nearly any subject imaginable and post your comments or questions. You can search on-line encyclopedias and other Internet sources for information you need to help you with your homework. You can read on-line newspapers. You can browse the World Wide Web for information on everything from popular musicians and television shows to ancient civilizations. You can even find Web pages that discuss the Internet itself and the issues that are involved with using and maintaining it.

Every Net citizen can make a contribution on the Internet. The student, the college professor, the space researcher, the senator, and everyone else who posts information on the Internet or communicates through its messaging systems are the people who make this marvelous new world we know as cyberspace such a special place to visit. They are shaping the Internet. They control what the Internet is as well as what it can be in the future.

That is the magic of the Internet.

2

How the Internet Is Changing Our Lives

"Just about every sector of society is being changed because of computer technology," proclaims David Allison, curator of the Division of Information Technology at the National Museum of American History.[1]

During the early years of the Internet's development, very few people had access to its resources. The Internet was strictly a world of computer experts and scientists. Only researchers and people who had connections to certain government or educational institutions were able to log on to it. At that time,

24

nearly all the information on the Internet was technically oriented.

But in the past several years, things have changed dramatically. Today, the Internet is filled with information on nearly every subject imaginable. You can look up information on your favorite rock band. You can take a virtual tour of the White House. You can even view paintings by master artists in museums around the world.

All the talk about the exciting things you can do on the Information Superhighway has led many people who had never thought of spending money for a home computer to purchase one—primarily for the purpose of going on the Internet. As people discovered how easy it was to get on the Internet, its influence on society increased. Before long, the Internet started to change the way people lived, worked, and spent their free time.

Elementary and Secondary Education

The Internet has developed into a wonderful tool for both students and teachers. A student who has an Internet connection at home, school, or in the library, can log on and get the information needed to complete homework assignments and other school projects. The amount of data stored in the Internet's computers is larger and more varied than the offerings of many school or public libraries.

Most teens find the Internet easy and exciting to use. Numerous databases and Web pages have been set up specifically for the purpose of helping young people find the information they want. And some popular Web browsers such as Yahoo list Internet sites that are of special interest to young people.

Teachers also use the Internet. They can locate lesson plans on a wide variety of topics. They can go on-line and communicate with other teachers and discuss how best to present material to their students. All sorts of materials are available to make lessons more exciting and easier to understand. According to Joe Panepinto, the executive editor of *FamilyPC* magazine, "Top teachers are using the Internet and World Wide Web to reinvigorate themselves and their classrooms so they can do what top teachers have always done: inspire a new generation of children to love learning."[2]

Malcolm Thomson, an astronomy teacher at Dalton School in New York City, is one educator who has discovered that the Internet can bring a new dimension of excitement into the classroom. He says, "Most of the explanations in astronomy emerge from observations over long periods. . . . Now you can compress the motions during those periods into a few seconds so you can conceptualize them."[3]

Thomson's students use their classroom Internet-connected computers to download images of planets, stars, and galaxies from NASA's Web site. And they use the Internet to access astronomy-related resources from all over the world. The class has a Web page where the course outline, assignments, and the students' work are posted.

These are only a few examples of how the

Internet can be used to add life and interest to school assignments. As more schools turn to the Internet as a teaching aid in the classroom, these benefits are sure to grow.

College On-Line

The Internet has also brought the resources of colleges and universities to more people. Students can now register for class, pay their tuition with a credit card, listen to lectures, and participate in on-line discussions through the magic of the Information Superhighway. Maria Newman, education writer for *The New York Times*, says,

> *Students who are not enrolled full time in such universities, and those who live far away from a particular university, can take their pick of a plethora [variety] of courses without ever setting foot on those campuses, if they have access to the Internet or the World Wide Web. No one knows how many on-line classes are being offered, but a search of the Web indicates that new ones are being added almost daily.*[4]

The Internet2 project, which is currently under development, will eventually make it possible for colleges and universities to make even better use of Internet technology as a teaching and research tool. The goals of the project—which includes over one hundred universities and educational computer networks—are to develop new applications such as real-time, multimedia collaboration, long-distance and lifelong learning programs, and other

THE U.S. Department of EDUCATION

Office of Educational Technology

Programs

State Regional Contacts

Federal Resources

E-Rate

Publications & Research

Conferences

Other

Education Technology Headlines...

The Clinton Administration has made an unprecedented commitment to bringing technology into the classroom. As a central element of the President's lifelong learning agenda, the Administration created the President's Educational Technology Initiative. Recognizing that technology can help expand opportunities for American children to improve their skills, maximize their potential, and ready them for the 21st century, President Clinton and Vice President Gore have challenged the nation to assure that all children are technologically literate by the dawn of the 21st century and equipped with the communication, math, science, reading, and critical thinking skills essential for enhancing learning and improving productivity and performance.

The Technology Literacy Challenge...

By logging on to <http://www.ed.gov/Technology>, students, teachers, and librarians can research information on how the Internet may benefit their schools.

applications that can bring college and university programs to more students.

Telecommuting

In recent years, many companies have started to allow their employees to work at home through the Internet. This is known as telecommuting.

"The very concept of 'going to work' is changing," declares Bill Montague, a writer with *USA Today*. "Modems have created telecommuters. They travel the information highway without leaving home or the kids. . . . Downtown skyscrapers grow emptier as rural states like Montana fill with telecommuters no longer tied to urban areas."[5]

Less than a decade ago, people who lived in rural areas had to move to the city if they wanted to work for big corporations. But telecommuting through the Internet offers people an alternative. If an Internet connection is available, people can now enjoy both the benefits of small-town life and a corporate paycheck.

Senator Conrad Burns of Montana is pushing for the government to help in bringing the information highway to people in rural areas of the nation. He described the benefits of working through the Internet this way in the *Congressional Record*:

> *Workers will travel to work on the information highways instead of our traditional highways. The cars on these information highways will be bits of information which can travel anywhere in the world instantly. . . . Think of it, a stockbroker could live in Circle, Montana, with a population of 931,*

Daryl Popkes enjoys the company of his cat as he works from home via the Internet.

and be in instant contact with anyone, anywhere, any way. That person wouldn't have to burn thousands of gallons of fossil fuel each year to drive to and from work. And best of all, that person would be able to work in rural America.[6]

Recreation

Ever since the Internet became available to the general public, it has been used for a wide variety of recreational activities. Steve Rimmer, author of *Planet Internet*, says, "Beyond its staggering capacity and limitless resources, the Internet is an interesting place to enjoy yourself. Like some enormous computer game, just when you think you've seen everything there is to see, a new facet of the Net will open up to you, and the adventure will begin again."[7] Browsing or "surfing" Web sites, multi-player games, on-line chats, as well as hobby-related Web sites and newsgroups have mushroomed in popularity in the past few years. The Internet's vast array of networks has made it possible to create countless sites for people all over the world who share common interests.

Music lovers, for example, can log on to the Internet and find information about their favorite recording artists. Many well-known entertainers have their own Web pages, and pages are posted by their fans as well. Photos, lyrics, tour information, and biographies of popular recording artists can be accessed through the Web. In addition to that, news-groups have been set up by fans of musical talents ranging from Weird Al Yankovic to classical com-posers such as Brahms and Beethoven. These newsgroups provide places for fans to go and discuss their favorite artists' recordings or performances.

Science-fiction fans can also find a wealth of material on the Internet about their futuristic interests. Suppose you are a *Star Trek* fan. You might want to start with the newsgroups that have been set up to discuss characters and story lines in the *Star Trek* universe. But that is only the beginning. If you look into the Internet a little deeper, you will discover the numerous Web pages, Internet forums, and chat groups available to Trekkies around the world.

Broadcasting over the Internet

For generations, teenagers have loved to listen to the radio. Now they can tune in to their favorite music, sports, or other radio fare over the Internet. With the help of programs such as RealAudio, hundreds of radio stations in the United States and Canada— as well as a multitude of foreign countries—can now be received by anyone with an Internet connection and a computer that has a sound card. A listing of these stations can be found at <http://www.radiotv.com>.

The Internet Multicasting Service was one of the first sites to offer Internet broadcasting services. In addition to conventional radio programs, it broadcasts programs of special interest to people who work with computers or who are employed by the computer industry. It also carries speeches by political leaders that might not be available from your local radio station. In addition to providing live programming, the Internet Multicasting Service records many of its transmissions and saves them in digital files. Internet users can download these files and listen to them at their convenience.[8]

A number of audio services that broadcast exclusively over the Internet have also come on-line. These include many specialty programs that might not find enough of an audience on a local station to justify their existence. In this way, the Internet gives

The Toshiba Infinia 7200 computer system includes a television receiver, FM radio tuner, telephone answering machine, and speakerphone.

an outlet to people who would not otherwise have the opportunity to make their voices and opinions heard.

In addition to that, many radio stations from other nations can be heard on the Internet. International shortwave stations such as the British Broadcasting Corporation, Voice of America, and Radio Moscow once had to depend on the right atmospheric conditions for their programs to reach listeners overseas. Now they, too, use the Internet to distribute their programming to listeners who live thousands of miles away. One good place to look for information about international radio stations that broadcast over the Internet is <http://www.dxing.com>.

Chatting on the Internet

With the Internet being a cutting-edge, worldwide communications medium, it is natural that people would want to use it to talk to each other. That explains why the Internet Relay Chat (IRC) is such a popular system. Internet chat rooms have been set up to accommodate people with any interest you can imagine. At any time you log on to the Internet, thousands of chat rooms are in operation. Day or night, you can go to an IRC room and make friends with other Internet users from around the globe.

Some on-line services, such as America Online and Prodigy have their own chat-room features. You can chat in groups, or chat one-to-one through the services of their private chat rooms and instant message systems. Web pages can also be designed to incorporate chat rooms. And some Internet chat rooms go one step further. They enable you to use a microphone and talk to your friends over the Internet, instead of having to type your messages on a keyboard. This makes chatting through the Internet almost like making a long-distance phone call—without having to pay a long-distance telephone company for the privilege. Also, there are programs on the market that allow you to make Internet phone calls to anyone in the world who has a similar computer program.

Communities in Cyberspace

In addition to casual chats, the Internet has provided the technology necessary to set up countless cybercommunities. These are not cities and towns that you can find on the map but communities in cyberspace, where people from any part of the world can come together to exchange ideas.

The Internet is full of virtual communities. Some are based on geographic location. Nearly every major city in the developed world has an Internet site where its cyber citizens can gather. Still other virtual communities are based on common interests and concerns. These communities are often made up of people from all over the country—if not from around the world.

Teenagers who have access to the Internet often enjoy being a part of a virtual community. Lindsey Andrews of Arnoldsville, Georgia, tells *USA Today*, "It's like an alternative world in some ways. . . . It's the same as having a big group of friends, but you don't see what anyone looks like. It's like the IDEAL that everyone speaks of when they say that you shouldn't judge people based on race, age, sex, etc."[9]

New virtual communities are coming on-line every day. After talking to people through the Internet and other computer networks for years, writer and Net citizen Howard Rheingold was inspired to set up an Internet community of his own—Electric Minds at <www.minds.com>. It was designed as a cyberspace village where people could really get to know each other and talk about common interests. As of late 1997, Electric Minds had over one hundred thousand registered members. While practically any topic can be discussed on Electric Minds' forums, many of the discussions have to do with the Internet, its social implications, and what directions it might take in the future.[10]

Although these virtual communities undoubtedly have many benefits, everyone is not so enthusiastic about them. Some feel that instead of bringing people together, Internet communities are isolating people into narrow groups that have little or no interest in activities outside of their own circle. David Shenk, author of *Data Smog: Surviving the Information Glut*, writes, "rather than our world becoming a cozy village, we are instead retreating into an electronic Tower of Babble, a global skyscraper. Instead of gathering us into the town square, the new information technology clusters us into social cubicles. There are fewer central spaces, and not even a common channel."[11]

Social Isolation

After a few trips on the Internet's Information Superhighway, it is easy to see how people can lose track of time there. You can spend hours going from one Web page or chat room to another without realizing how much time has passed. No one can deny that the Internet offers computer users a fascinating world of discovery. Once you have signed on to this worldwide communications system, there seems to be no end to the Web pages, newsgroups, chats, and other exciting areas you can explore.

As with anything else, there is a downside to spending too much time logged on to the Internet. There are only so many hours in a day. When people spend the majority of their free time "surfing the Web," browsing through newsgroups, or chatting on the Internet, they no longer have time for real life friends and neighbors or other activities that they once enjoyed.

Teenagers who spend much of their free time in cyberspace often argue that if it was not for the Internet, they would probably spend most of their weekends and evenings watching television. Many parents agree. In a letter to *USA Today*, David and Marcia Geoff said of their teenager's Internet use: "We have noticed that the use of the Internet has led to less time in front of the TV. This seems like a good tradeoff."[12]

That may well be true in many cases. Interacting with other people on the Internet or browsing through the Internet's vast storehouse of information is undoubtedly a better use of time than sitting in front of the television. Still, there is cause for concern when people are truly addicted to the Internet.

Ironically, the Internet is also used as a meeting place by those who want to discuss their Internet addictions. Rick Barrette, an Ohio University graduate student, started the Webaholics home page when two of his classmates dropped out of school after spending too much time on the World Wide Web.

One message posted anonymously on the site read: "The Web has practically ruined my life. I once actually used to be popular and good at sports. . . . [Now] I have no friends, a bad attitude, and my grades dropped big time. I also get eye strain from staring at the screen for such periods of time."[13]

The line between addiction and heavy use can be hard to draw. But the problem of Internet addiction is now taken seriously by most mental health professionals. The main fear psychology experts have is that some people are becoming so involved with their Internet activities that they are socially isolating themselves. Their excessive time on the Internet can keep them away from friends, family, and people in their own community. These experts stress that it is important for everyone—especially young people—to maintain a healthy balance between the hours they spend on the Internet and the time they spend in face-to-face contact with friends and family.

What Can You Do to Cut Back?

People who find themselves spending too much time on the Internet at home can take several measures to cut back. Here are a few suggestions:

- Limit yourself to spending only so much time on the Internet a day. If you find you lose track of time, set an alarm clock or timer.

- Ask yourself if the things you are doing on the Internet are really worth the amount of time they involve. Also, are they worth the time they take away from other activities you enjoy?

- If the person you are going to E-mail or have an Internet chat with lives nearby, consider calling them on the phone or visiting them instead.

As we move into the new millennium, the Internet is certain to change our lives in ways no one could predict. The challenge for government, business, and individual Net citizens is to keep these changes positive.

3

Who Controls the Internet?

The Internet is the most democratic of all media. This global computerized communications system is made up of thousands of independent sites. The Internet is set up in such a way that no single entity is in control of the entire system. Anyone connected to the Internet can post a message to a newsgroup, set up a Web page, or express a viewpoint in Internet chats or forums.

Misinformation

The fact that anyone can post to the Internet has made it a spawning ground

40

for all kinds of rumors and outright lies. Urban myths (stories about fictitious events) and other untruths that would normally take years to spread by word of mouth can circle the globe in seconds if they are posted on the Internet.

Misinformation on the Internet is not hard to find. Newsgroups and Web pages have been set up to discuss every conspiracy theory known to humankind. Everything from urban myths to government cover-ups and "the real truth" about UFOs can be seen on the Internet.

Incidents that have no rational explanation have always bred myths. People want to at least think they know the cause of happenings that seem to defy explanation. The crash of TWA Flight 800 in 1996 is one example of such an incident. When government investigators could find no apparent cause for the jet's crash, Internet users began posting conjectures about what "really happened." Laurrel Merlindo wrote in an article for *Computer Life* magazine, "The true cause of the crash is the topic of as many theories as the assassination of JFK. How many of us received that 'official military document' stating that the plane was accidentally downed by a United States warship launching a practice missile at the wrong time?"[1]

Before news stories are released through radio, television, magazines, and newspapers, the facts are checked by experienced editors. On the Internet, most of the information you see has not been put through the same process. People who are accustomed to obtaining their news from the pre-edited commercial media, such as radio, television, and news magazines, can be fooled by deceptive postings. At times, even the most experienced in our society can be misled by misinformation.

Browsing through conspiracy theories on the Internet can be fun. But when you use the Internet to look up information that is important to you, it is wise to make sure it comes from a reputable source. Just remember, many postings that you see in newsgroups are often nothing more than personal opinions, even when they are written as though they are facts. Web sites operated by reliable news sources, such as those run by newspapers, magazines, news services, and television networks are the best choices for accurate information.

The Dark Side of the Internet

While the Internet is an exciting place to explore, there are dangers that users should be aware of. In the United States, the Internet is not regulated by the government. This, along with the fact that it is so easy to hide your true identity on the Internet, has made it attractive to people involved in many different kinds of criminal activity. Susan Grant, director of the consumer watchdog group Internet Fraud Watch, cautions, "I think that a lot of people have this vision of the Internet as being a wonderful place—which it is—but it's got some really dark back alleys to it."[2]

In addition to outright criminal activity, materials that many people find objectionable are available through the Internet. Pornography and instructions on how to make drugs and bombs can be posted on the Internet as easily as a cake recipe or a request for information needed for a homework assignment. In recent years, police departments across the nation have come across cases in which criminals used the Internet or information posted there to help them commit their crimes. These crimes include computer hacking, picking locks, and other illegal activities.

Young people often know more about the Internet than their parents. Still, young people are often the victims of Internet-related crimes. In recent years, there have been cases where child molesters used the Internet to contact children, whom they later abused. Many times, child molesters have found their victims in chat rooms, where it is very easy for a person to hide his or her identity and to pretend to be someone he or she is not.

In one case in 1997, Samuel Manzie, a fourteen-year-old boy who lived in Jackson Township, New Jersey, was lured into an encounter with a forty-three-year-old man he met in an America Online chat room. Later, Samuel was charged for sexually assaulting and murdering Edward Werner, an eleven-year-old neighbor who had been selling candy door-to-door to raise money for a school project.

America Online spokesperson Tricia Primrose

warned, "The online world is not immune to people with less than good intentions any more than the offline world is. The same rules apply: Don't talk to strangers. Don't give out your personal information. And don't agree to meet somebody without telling a parent or going with a parent."[3]

Scams

The Internet has also become a haven for con artists. Hardly anyone who has been on-line for long can open their E-mail without finding pitches for everything from fraudulent work-at-home opportunities and pyramid schemes to raffles (contests that require a fee to enter) or deals on computer equipment that sound too good to be true. Margaret Mannix, a business and technology writer for *U.S. News & World Report*, says, "One work-at-home scheme, for example, advertises that you can make lots of money designing graphics on your home computer. But you must first send in $300 to $500 for the graphic software."[4]

As more people flock to the Internet, so will criminals who want to take advantage of them. According to Wisconsin attorney general James Doyle, "It's the growth area. It [the Internet] is something that is going to make the mail and telephone look like old-fashioned devices."[5] A number of these scam operators have been apprehended by police. But for every one that is caught, many more are prowling the Internet for victims.

Federal Bureau of Investigation Educational Web Publication

Safety Tips for Kids
on the Internet

Should you become aware of the transmission, use, or viewing of child pornography while online, immediately report this to your local FBI Office or to the National Center for Missing and Exploited Children by calling 1-800-843-5678

Safety Tips

- Never give out identifying information such as Name, Home Address, School Name, or Telephone Number in a public message such as at a chat room or on bulletin boards. Never send a person a picture of you without first checking with your parent or guardian.

- Never respond to essages or bulletin board items that are:
  - Suggestive
  - Obscene
  - Belligerent
  - Threatening
  - Make You Feel Uncomfortable

- Be careful when someone offers you something for nothing, such as gifts and money. Be very careful about any offers that involve your coming to a meeting or having someone visit your house.

- Tell your parent or guardian right away if you come across any information that makes you feel uncomfortable.

- Never arrange a face to face meeting without telling your parent or guardian. If your parent or guardian agree to the meeting, make sure that you meet in a public place and have a parent or guardian with you.

- Remember that people online may not be who they seem. Because you can't see or even hear the person it would be easy for someone to misrepresent him- or herself. Thus, someone indicating that "she" is a "12-year-old-girl" could in reality be an older man.

- Be sure that you are dealing with someone that you and your parents know and trust before giving out any personal information about yourself via E-mail.

- Get to know your "online friends" just as you get to know all of your other friends.

The Federal Bureau of Investigation offers these tips for safely surfing the Web at <http://www.fbi.gov/kids/ internet/internet.htm>.

Reaching the Youth Market

While adults are the target of the bulk of on-line swindles, teenagers have also been drawn into schemes that operate through the Internet. Sometimes, scam operators encourage teens and children to enter their parent's credit card number in order to "win a prize" or "confirm their identity."

There is also some concern about how a number of legitimate businesses use the Internet to market to young people. In 1996, nearly 4 million people under age seventeen signed on to the Internet, many from middle- and upper-income families. This new influx of young consumers to cyberspace has prompted marketers to rush on to the Internet as well.

Marketers who want to reach young people use the Internet in a variety of ways. Some companies use their Web sites to introduce new products. Others may encourage children who visit to keep buying until they own the entire collection of dolls or toy race cars that the company offers. David Leonhardt, a writer for *Business Week* magazine, reports, "By limiting the number of each new Beanie Baby and announcing on its Web site which dolls it had discontinued, Ty Inc. in Oak Brook, Ill., for example, cashed in on the desire of 7-year-olds to collect."[6]

Sometimes, Web sites designed to attract children not only sell products but also gather information about children and their families. Larry Armstrong, another writer for *Business Week*, says, "One of the oldest kids' sites, from Web site developer Kidscom Co. in Milwaukee, asked registrants for personal information about themselves and their families from which it culled statistics for advertisers. Grey Advertising Inc. set up a kids' site purely for marketing research, soliciting info from children about their sneakers, cool words, and favorite music."[7] On-line chats are also used to gather marketing information about young people and their buying habits.

This type of activity has prompted the Consumer Federation of America and other watchdog groups to call for government guidelines for how the Internet can be used for market research, especially when children and teenagers are involved.

Pornography

Sexually oriented material makes up only a small portion of what is available on the Internet. Nevertheless, it has caused a great deal of controversy in recent years. No one is forced to read pornographic newsgroups or visit sexually explicit Web sites. But these materials can be accessed by Internet users who choose to view them—and by children and teenagers. And that has caused a great deal of concern among parents, teachers, and religious organizations.

Gus Venditto, a writer for *Internet World* magazine, says, "Few parents—no matter how liberal their political views—want their children exposed to some of the material that's freely available at the fringe of the Internet. No educator can deny the problem: With just a few clicks, a youngster can summon images that would be ruled offensive by any school board anywhere."[8]

Sexually explicit newsgroups can usually be identified by their titles—such as alt.sex, alt.sex.stories, and alt.sex.wanted. As of late 1997, nothing had been done to prevent children and teens from accessing them. According to *U.S. News & World Report* writer Randall E. Stross, "Anyone who has spent five minutes using a 'news reader' would have no difficulty locating, for example, the 250 or so naughty public newsgroups and all are as accessible to an intrepid 10-year-old as an adult."[9]

Some Web sites that contain sexual materials have a policy that requires Web surfers to declare that they are twenty-one years or older before they enter. However, there is no way to make sure that people entering the site are telling the truth about their ages.

Chat areas on the Internet also pose a concern. While some chat rooms and forums are identified as being sexually oriented, sexually explicit conversations can take place in almost any chat room. Even chat rooms that have been designated for children are not entirely safe. Child molesters have been known to lurk in these areas. Often, they pose as teenagers so they can gain their victims' trust more easily.

Hate Groups

A multitude of hate groups have moved onto the Internet since the early 1990s. Organizations such as the National Alliance, the Ku Klux Klan, the Socialist White People's Party, and a variety of other white supremacy groups have pages on the World Wide Web. And they frequently use E-mail and other Internet services to exchange information and to attempt to recruit new members.

The power of the Internet offers hate groups a relatively inexpensive way to reach a potential audience of millions of people—many of whom would otherwise have been unreachable. The cost of having a Web site on the Internet is well within the reach of nearly any organization that seeks exposure.

Rabbi Abraham Cooper of the Simon Wiesenthal Center estimates that hate groups and fringe religious organizations now have over five hundred Web sites. And that number seems to be growing. The reason, Rabbi Cooper asserts, is economic. "Why put fliers under windshield wipers when for a few dollars more, you could go to the Web?"[10]

Many hate groups are open about their prejudice and hatred toward African Americans, Jews, gays, and others. Other hate groups are more subtle. They claim they do not hate anyone. They try to present their organizations to potential members as defenders of the white race—similar to organizations that defend minority races in America, such as the NAACP. Still other hate groups claim to be Christian and base their prejudice and hatred of people of other races and faiths on religious grounds.

All hate groups do have one thing in common. They are always on the lookout for new recruits. Many are especially interested in bringing teenagers into their folds. A spokesperson for the Simon Wiesenthal Center said, "In all these cases, the rhetoric and visuals are not new. What is new is the opportunity to cheaply, effectively and directly market hate to a coveted audience—the young, who are the heaviest users of cyberspace."[11]

Cults

In addition to hate groups, religious cults use the Internet to reach people. The Heaven's Gate cult, whose leader, Marshall Applewhite, and thirty-eight other members committed suicide in March 1997, was one such group. Their Web page, which explained the group's beliefs and philosophy, was designed to attract potential members.

Yvonne McCurdy-Hill was one person who was convinced to join Heaven's Gate through their Internet campaign. McCurdy-Hill, a mother of five who lived in Cincinnati, left her children to join the cult after learning about it through the Internet.

While adults are sometimes lured into cults through the Internet, teenagers can be even more susceptible. This is especially true of teens who come from broken families. Tal Brooke, editor of the book *Virtual Gods*, argues, "I think the Net can be an effective cult recruiting tool. It's like fishing with a lure—Little Johnny Latchkey gets behind the keyboard and hears someone say, 'I'm the dad you never had.'"[12]

Fortunately, not all cult efforts to recruit new members over the Internet are successful. In September 1996, the Heaven's Gate cult posted a recruitment message in dozens of Internet newsgroups. The message said in part, "Time to die for God?. . . Whether we like it or not, the Armageddon—the Mother of Holy Wars—has begun, and it will not cease until the plowing under is completed."[13] But the Heaven's Gate cult did not get the results it expected. In fact, most of the messages they received mocked their posting.

Is Censorship the Answer?

The influx of pornography, hate groups, crime, fast-money schemes, and other unscrupulous activities on the Internet has caused a great deal of concern in recent years. It has given rise to debates about whether the Internet should be regulated. The question is, Should a government agency take charge of what goes through the Internet? Or should the Net remain the most unregulated electronic communications media in the world?

People who want government censorship of the Internet feel that it is in the public interest to restrict the availability of certain types of materials. A brochure published by the National Coalition for the Protection of Children and Families said,

> *[The Internet contains] everything explicit that can be imagined and many other types of material that are beyond the comprehension of most Americans. . . . For the first time in history, we are giving young children unlimited access to pornography, with no age check and no responsibility/verification procedures in place. This has never occurred in the print, broadcast, satellite or cable media before.*[14]

Censorship of Internet content has been attempted in other parts of the world. In the nation of Singapore, for example, the Singapore Broadcast Authority has control over the Internet—much as the Federal Communications Commission has control over radio and TV transmissions in the United States. In Singapore, anyone who wants to be an

Internet provider must register with the government, as do owners of Web pages that contain political or religious information. The Singapore Broadcast Authority has the power to force Internet service providers to block any Web sites it determines are objectionable. If the providers refuse to do so, they can be fined or their license to provide Internet service can be revoked.

Karen M. Sorensen, an on-line researcher for Human Rights Watch, says that the Singapore government prohibits sites "that bring the government into hatred or contempt or which excite disaffection against the government . . . [and] undermine public confidence in the administration of justice."[15]

Even with these regulations in place, the Singapore Broadcast Authority admits that it will not be able to completely control the Internet sites that Singapore citizens can access.[16]

The Case Against Censorship

While some people are fighting to keep offensive materials off the Internet, others contend that the Internet should not be censored at all. They assert that everyone should have the right to free expression on the Internet—even if the material they post is upsetting or disgusting to the majority of Internet users.

In the United States, a number of organizations, including the Electronic Frontier Foundation and the American Civil Liberties Union (ACLU), firmly believe that the First Amendment rights of free speech would be violated if laws controlling Internet content are passed. Barry S. Steubhardt, associate director of the ACLU said of the attempts to censor Internet content, "The restrictions are worrisome first of all because we, as Americans, believe very strongly in the principles of free speech. . . . We believe that they are universal principles, and that government should not be censoring our freedom of speech."[17]

Arguments against government censorship of the Internet include

- The First Amendment's protection of free speech must be upheld.

- The type of undesirable information some people want to censor would still be available to anyone who wants it, since books that explain how to commit nearly any type of crime are available in the United States.

- Hate groups can and do openly spread their messages through print media and radio, and restricting Internet content will not prevent them from doing so.

- Pornography is available in a wide variety of media to anyone over twenty-one years old who wants to buy it.

The main reasons the Internet is not regulated in the United States by the Federal Communications Commission (FCC), like television and radio transmissions, are

- Unlike television and radio, the Internet does not transmit material over the public airwaves.

- The Internet offers information only if a user requests it.

- It is difficult for Internet users to accidentally stumble onto pornographic pictures or other offensive material they do not wish to see.

- Parents can purchase software to block sites they do not want their children to visit.

Rachelle Chong is the first FCC commissioner to actively use the Internet. She enjoys "surfing the Web" and has taken part in on-line discussions concerning the Internet's use and its future. Commissioner Chong argues,

> *The Internet has been the tremendous success that it's been because the government has kept its mitts off it. I'm in the camp that government should not regulate unless it has to. For example, the Communications Decency Act [passed by congress in 1996 but overturned by a federal court] was not the right way to regulate the Internet. The better way to control [the Internet] is with software controls, and, frankly, parental responsibility has got to be the key.*[18]

The Communications Decency Act

The Communications Decency Act, which was part of the Telecommunications Act of 1996, was the first federal law to try to censor sexually explicit and other objectionable material on the Internet. The act

Rachelle Chong is one of the first FCC commissioners to make use of the Internet.

established criminal penalties for the transmission over the Internet of certain types of indecent materials, such as child pornography and explicit adult sexual material. United States senator James Exon, the sponsor of this bill, said, "Many critics say that on the Internet, anything should go, no matter how outrageous. I say the framers of the Constitution never intended for the First Amendment to protect pornographers and pedophiles."[19]

The Communications Decency Act received support from conservative organizations such as the Christian Coalition and the Family Research Council. These groups argued that protecting children from indecent material was more important than protecting the free speech rights of those who wanted to post or view pornography on the Internet.

Not everyone was pleased with the passage of this act. Opponents of the bill claimed the language was too vague and the law would be difficult to enforce. Also, the Communications Decency Act established criminal penalties for the mere transmission of certain materials—which could possibly make criminals out of anyone who ran an Internet service or bulletin-board system on which someone else posted this material. Within days after the decency act was passed it was challenged in court.

On June 12, 1996, a three-judge United States Federal District Court panel in Pennsylvania overturned the Communications Decency Act. Their ruling stated that the act was unconstitutional, and they declared that the Internet deserves the highest possible level of protection from government intrusion. Judge Stewart Dalzell, one of the federal judges who ruled on the matter, wrote, "Just as the strength of the Internet is chaos, so the strength of our liberty depends upon the chaos and cacophony of the unfettered speech the First Amendment protects."[20]

The U.S. Justice Department appealed the case to the Supreme Court. On June 26, 1997, the Supreme Court unanimously decided that the Communications Decency Act was unconstitutional. This decision *(Reno* v. *ACLU)* granted people who use the Internet the same free speech protection that already exists for authors and publishers of print mediums such as books and magazines.

The fight over censorship of the Internet in America did not end with the court decision against the Communications Decency Act. Several states have their own censorship laws on the books, and others are in the process of passing laws that would prohibit the posting of pornography and other materials deemed offensive. Some of these laws, including a New York State law that was similar to the Communications Decency Act, have already been overturned. Despite these decisions, the battle over what can legally be transmitted over the Internet is likely to continue for some time.

Access-Blocking Software

Methods of filtering offensive Internet content are already available to those who want it. Most on-line services, such as America Online, Prodigy, and CompuServe, provide controls that allow parents to limit the Internet sites that their children can access. Families that have a direct Internet connection can buy software such as Net Nanny. This and similar programs block access to materials that parents do not want their children to view.

Most access-blocking programs allow parents to set the blocking action at any level they wish. Access to Web pages, newsgroups, chat rooms, and other Internet sites can be blocked if certain key words appear, such as adult, sex, drugs, bombs, or swear words. The filters in this software can also be set to prevent young Internet users from giving out personal information, such as their phone number or home address.

The manufacturers of Net Nanny said about their product,

> Net Nanny allows the parent to have full discretion over which content, material, words, phrases, Internet sites or URLs are to be monitored and blocked. The toolkit gives parents the ability to impose their individual values in their respective households. [It] puts the power of control in the hands of parents, schools and employers—not regulators. In this way, the Internet, with all its positive attributes, remains a source for uncensored information.[21]

No matter how well it is designed, no program is capable of blocking everything that a parent might not want a child or teenager to view. On occasion, such postings can be found in otherwise "safe" areas

Net Nanny software claims to protect children, corporations, and freedom of speech on the Internet.

of the Internet. If the writer has carefully avoided using key words that many access-blocking software programs scan for, offensive material can slip through.

In all, these programs are reasonably effective in protecting children from the dark side of the Internet. But they have created some controversies of their own. Several access-blocking programs not only prevent young people from visiting forbidden sites but also keep a record of all the Internet sites that children have entered or attempted to enter. This approach, some feel, goes too far in supervising young people's Internet activities. Langdon Winner writes in the February/March 1997 issue of *Technology Review* magazine, "Products of this kind remind one of the totalitarian states earlier this century that tried to establish order by getting family members to spy on each other."[22]

While access-blocking software can make parents feel at ease about what their children might find on the Internet, it can also cause a great deal of stress in the family. The fact that parents buy and install such programs often causes young people to feel insulted that their parents do not trust them. *Wired* magazine columnist Jon Katz says of his teenage daughter,

> She has been online since she was 10. We have never thought of acquiring blocking software, which would be offensive and demeaning to her, but she's been taught not to pass around her name, address, or phone number—and to pass problems or unsettling experiences onto us. . . .

We need to teach ourselves how to trust children to make rational judgments about their own safety. Instead of holding them back, we should be pushing them forward. Instead of shielding them, we should take them by the hand, guide them to the gate, and cheer them on.[23]

Dealing with Internet Crime

When criminal activity does take place over the Internet, censorship opponents argue, laws that are already in effect can be used to prosecute it. Child pornography on the Internet is one such activity. People who handle such material can already be punished under laws that make the possession of this material illegal, whether it is posted on the Internet or viewed at home in the form of photographs or videos.

Even if laws were passed that forbid certain types of material to be posted on the Internet, imposing such censorship would not be easy. Because the Internet is a global communications system, many experts consider unrealistic the idea of the United States or any other nation passing laws to control its content. The reason is simple. People who wish to engage in an Internet activity that is illegal in the United States can easily set up a Web site in a nation that allows such activities. That would, in effect, put them outside the jurisdiction of American courts.

Hard-core pornography is an industry that is run mainly from foreign countries. By giving out their credit card numbers and paying a fee, Internet users can access pornographic materials that may well be illegal to sell or possess in their own community. Much of the on-line pornography industry is based in Europe and the Caribbean.

Controversies such as these have caused some people to push for an international policy to control how the Internet is used. While many governments would prefer that Internet users in their country not have access to certain objectionable materials, it would indeed be difficult to convince all governments to agree on uniform censorship goals.

What do you think? Should people be allowed to decide for themselves what to view on the Internet? Or should America's lawmakers attempt to control Internet content that they feel is harmful to the nation's population?

4

Security on the Internet

Any individual, institution, or business that has computer systems connected to the outside world via a phone line is a potential target of computer crime. Among the greatest worries are hackers and viruses.

Hackers

Originally, the word *hacker* meant someone who was clever enough to make computers do things that no one else had thought of. But today, a hacker generally means someone who breaks into other people's computer systems.

Hackers have many motives for their

actions. Many just want to break into computers to prove they can do it or to explore the system and its capabilities. They are motivated by the challenge of outwitting systems that should be secure. Other hackers have more sinister motives—such as stealing information, destroying data, or stopping a computer system from functioning. This type of hacker is sometimes referred to as a "cracker."

One of the first computer hacking incidents to grab the national media's attention occurred on November 2, 1988. Robert Tappan Morris, a student at Cornell University in Ithaca, New York, went into the school's computer room and typed a "worm"—a program designed to duplicate itself but not destroy data—into the university's computer system.

Morris programmed his worm to do the following things: duplicate itself hundreds of times; search out the names of all system users, as well as their passwords; send copies of the original program to every other computer it could reach; and relay the information back to him.

But Morris made a small mistake in the program. He put a decimal point in the wrong place. And on account of this mistake, the worm reproduced much more quickly than he expected. Once Morris's worm entered a computer, it would copy itself over and over until the computer could no longer function.

Morris's worm not only spread through Cornell University's computers but throughout the Internet as well. This ultimately affected approximately

85,200 computer users—including government agencies, businesses, and researchers. While the worm did not destroy any data, it caused a multitude of problems for every computer user who came in contact with it. Work was disrupted for up to a week while computer experts labored to remove the worm from the system. And the security of the network itself was compromised.

Morris later said that the worm was released only as an experiment. He did not intend to harm anyone's computer data. But his experiment proved to be very expensive. The Computer Virus Industry Association estimated that the employee-hours needed to remove the worm program from the system as well as the lost work time on infected computers added up to more than $98 million.[1]

As a result of his experiment, Morris was expelled from Cornell University. And in July 1989, he was the first person to be charged under the 1986 Computer Fraud and Abuse Act—a federal law that makes it a crime to enter a computer system you have not been authorized to use. The jury found Morris guilty. He was fined $10,000 and was sentenced to three years probation and four hundred hours of community service.[2]

Protecting Computer Data

No one wants unauthorized people to view private data in their computers. But people who operate a business or order merchandise over the Internet have another concern. Credit card numbers that are sent over the Internet can be stolen if a hacker is able to intercept them. There are some safeguards that can be taken to help keep hackers out of a computer system. They include passwords, firewalls, and encryption systems.

Passwords

Many computer and Internet users employ a password to protect the information they have stored in their computer. Passwords are also used to keep unauthorized people from using your Internet account. A password is made up of a combination of letters, numbers, or both.

If a password is to be effective, it should be difficult for an unauthorized person to guess. For example, you should not use your name, address, or phone number as a password. The more complicated a password is, the more security it provides. Also, a password should not be any word or number that appears in a dictionary, newspaper, or telephone book. Hackers can set up their computers to try millions of guesses from lists of commonly used passwords.

Finally, a password should only be known to the person who uses it. If you use more than one Internet service or bulletin board, it is a good idea to use a separate password for each account.

Firewalls

The term *firewall* refers to software or hardware barriers that can be put up between computer systems and the Internet. Firewalls help control who can access your computer systems. They can also control what is transmitted from your computer system to the Internet. According to Garry S. Howard, author of the book *Introduction to Internet Security: From Basics to Beyond*, "Internet firewalls are the most comprehensive tool to implement an organization's network security. With firewalls established between corporation and public, activity at every level can be monitored, greatly reducing the chances of infiltration, vandalism, theft, or unauthorized use of the system."[3]

But firewalls also have a negative side. Because of the extra information processing involved with using a firewall, they slow down network traffic. They also give any person who is in charge of operating the firewall the opportunity to completely monitor and record all Internet traffic that flows through the system. In addition to that, firewalls provide an attractive target for hackers, who are in some cases able to bypass them.

Encryption Systems

Concerns about security on the Internet have prompted some computer users to encrypt, or scramble, data before they send it through the Internet. This makes it difficult, if not impossible, for unauthorized people to read the message should they intercept it. Encryption programs work in the following way: The person who sends the encrypted message and the person who receives it have a key or password that allows them to unscramble the data and read it in plain English.

Encryption is especially important when financial transactions or credit card numbers are transmitted over the Internet. "Cryptography [encryption] is crucial because it provides the only means for protecting customers and companies from electronic eavesdropping," states Edmund L. Andrews, a reporter with *The New York Times*.[4]

Unfortunately, there are drawbacks to encryption programs being so widely available. Hate groups, terrorists, and people involved in organized crime commonly use encryption systems to make it difficult for law enforcement officials to monitor their sometimes criminal Internet communications.

Because of these concerns, laws have been passed in the United States forbidding the export of encryption programs that are extremely difficult to decode. However, many people question the value of this law, because similar programs are still being produced and sold in other parts of the world.

Is Computer Data Ever Completely Safe?

Even when all possible safety measures are taken, there is no guarantee that a hacker or cracker cannot gain entry to a computer system that is attached to the Internet or to a telephone line. Even computers belonging to the United States government have been attacked.

In 1995, for example, Wendell Dingus found a way to obtain the log-in passwords to computers that belonged to the U.S. Air Force and NASA. Once he had those passwords, he was able to access data from the U.S. Air Force Information Warfare Center and other computers that contained classified defense information. Eventually, he was caught. When the case went to court in 1997, Dingus was fined $40,000 to pay for the time and effort it had cost the government to track him down.

Concern about Viruses

Even before the Internet came into widespread public use, computer users had reason to be concerned about picking up a virus. Any computer user who downloaded program files from a bulletin board faced the risk of picking up a virus, which could wipe out data or make his or her equipment malfunction. You could also infect your computer with a virus if you borrowed a disk from a friend whose computer had been infected.

But the Internet has made it possible for viruses to spread faster than they ever could before. Once infected material has been posted to the Internet, it can be transmitted anywhere in the world within a matter of seconds. In a survey conducted by the National Computer Security Association (NSCN) in 1996, 90 percent of corporations had been affected by one or more computer viruses in the preceding year.[5]

What Is a Computer Virus?

A computer virus is a digital code or program created to cause problems in other people's computer systems. A virus spreads by attaching itself to computer files and reproducing itself. After viruses attach themselves to one file, they often go on to duplicate themselves onto other files and programs in the machine. This is known as a virus infection.

Since the beginning of the computer revolution, thousands of viruses have been identified. Some viruses were created as pranks. They cause strange things to happen when certain programs are run, such as making letters in a document "fall" to the bottom of the screen or causing text to turn upside down. When multimedia computers (which can play music and sounds through their speakers) became popular in the mid-1990s, viruses were created to cause programs to make strange sounds, randomly play music, or do other odd things.

But other viruses are far more malicious. They were designed to get into a computer system and cause as much damage as possible: erasing files, jamming up computer systems so they will not function, or scrambling data to the point that it is unreadable. These are the viruses that computer users fear most.

Why would anyone want to create such malicious viruses? The reasons probably vary as much as the types of damage the viruses produce. Perhaps the virus was created to harm a person whom the virus writer disliked by messing up his or her computer. Perhaps the virus creator was angry at a former employer and wanted to destroy all the data in the company's computer system. Perhaps a virus was written by a student who wanted to cause havoc with school computers. But once a virus has been created and distributed, it seldom stops at its intended target's computer.

Types of Viruses

There are several categories of computer viruses. File infectors are viruses that attach themselves to computer programs and run every time that program is executed. Cluster infector viruses do not attach themselves to programs but modify the file system so that they are run before other programs. System infector viruses reside in the boot sector of computer disks and go to work every time the disk is used to boot (start up) the system.

New Virus Threats

Up until the mid-1990s, people who only received and transmitted text files through the Internet felt relatively safe from computer virus attacks. That changed when a new strain of viruses was developed that can be transmitted along with documents prepared in Microsoft's MS Word, one of the most popular brands of word-processing software. These are known as macro viruses because they attach themselves to the macro part of the file. A macro is a set of instructions that is carried out when the computer operator presses a certain key or combination of keys. Macro viruses can also be programmed to go into effect automatically when the file is opened.

According to Kenneth R. van Wyk, a technical director with Science Applications International Corp., "As application programs have become increasingly powerful, their macro languages have enabled the user to perform more and more tasks. So, if a malicious person could somehow trick a user into running a malicious macro, the program could alter and even delete that user's files. Almost nothing stands in the way."[6]

Trojan Horse

This type of program pretends to accomplish one task while it is actually performing another. Trojan horses are not classified as viruses because they do not attempt to reproduce themselves, but most Trojan horses are malicious. One example of a Trojan horse is a fake log-in program that collects passwords and other account information and then delivers the data to the programmer. Another example would be a game that collects information from your hard disk while you play it and later returns that information to a specific E-mail address.

Worm

A worm is similar to a virus in the way it replicates itself. Only, it is a stand-alone program that does not need to attach itself to another file in order to spread. A worm can stop a computer system by making so many copies of itself that it completely fills the system's memory. While data is usually not destroyed, a worm infection can be costly to eradicate from computer systems.

Preventing Virus Attacks

Every year, corporations spend billions of dollars attempting to prevent viruses from infecting their computer systems. While many of their efforts would be impractical for the average computer user, there are things that everyone can do to lessen the risk of virus attacks.

One important step in fighting this problem is to invest in a good virus-scanning software program. These programs check any file that you download for possible virus infection. They will also check through your computer's existing files for viruses, worms, or suspicious changes in data. A number of such programs are available for both IBM-type and Apple computers. Some are even able to repair much of the damage that a virus has already done to computer files.

However, as computer professionals find methods of successfully exterminating viruses that are currently being transmitted through the Internet, virus writers are busy developing new ones. Because of that, nearly all the major companies that sell virus-scanning software offer updates that cover the latest threats to your valuable computer data.

Even the best virus-scanning programs and their updates can not offer you a 100 percent guarantee against virus infection. So it is important to make backup copies of important files on separate disks.

Virus Hoaxes

A number of hoaxes concerning viruses that can supposedly be transmitted through E-mail have been circulating through the Internet in the past few years. People have received messages telling them that they should never open any E-mail with certain phrases such as "GOOD TIMES" or "JOIN THE CREW" in the subject line. If they do, they are warned, a malicious virus will invade their computer and damage the machine, destroy data, or do both.

Ellen Grant, writer for *Info Security Magazine*, counters,

> *Viruses and Trojans don't leak out of emails—they can't. If you get something [an e-mail message] telling you that your hard drive is going to melt. It's a hoax. If it's a message with the word WARNING and three exclamation marks—it's a hoax. If it tells you to pass this on to all your friends—it's a hoax—don't pass it on. If it says "THIS IS NOT A JOKE!!!" it is almost certainly someone's idea of a joke.* [7]

However, E-mail attachments—files that are sent through the Internet attached to E-mail messages—can transmit viruses as easily as any other file. So it's always a good idea to run a virus scan on them.

A good place to find information on computer virus hoaxes and other myths that are spread through the Internet is
<http://www.kumite.com/myths>.

http://www.kumite.com/myths

Computer Virus Myths

Confirmed. Houston. The sky is not falling.

No joke! Symantec paid Elvira to talk about computer viruses

Rob Rosenberger, webmaster (updated 2/10/1998)
This site contains no paid ads and sells no products

Attention cartoonists! If you joked about computer viruses in a strip, submit it for the 1998 Computer Virus Hysteria Awards! Internet users will vote in May for their favorite comic strip...

"Mundus vult decipi"
(the world wants to be deceived)

Read all about computer virus myths & hoaxes

The specific reason why this web site exists. Learn about the myths, the hoaxes, the urban legends, and the implications of computer virus myths. You can also see a list of virus hoaxes from A to Z.

2/7/98 news flash
A new variant of the "*Join the Crew*" alert says the mythical virus can destroy a Cisco router. Ironically, this variant alert seems to have started when a well-meaning Cisco employee forwarded the warning to a list of clients...

⚠ **Latest fad: "combination alerts."** The newest chain letters combine multiple hoaxes in a single message. One alert warns people not to read email containing either 'Join the Crew' or 'Penpal Greetings' in the subject line. Another warns people to delete messages without reading them if they contain any of *four* evil phrases in the subject line. These combination-alert chain letters grew *really* popular, *really* fast...

"Why would the author not just make the subject 'New virus alert!'? Everyone would open it and the dragon would pop out and eat your computer."
-- *Usenet reader Keith Varnes, asking the obvious question*

New stuff, recent flare-ups

- Newest hoaxes
  - *Win a Holiday* virus
  - Yahoo! world domination virus
  - Bill Gates $1,000 virus (a.k.a. *EEVP* virus or embedded executable virus program)
  - A.I.D.S. virus (aka *Open Very Cool* virus)
  - AOL v4.0 cookie Trojan
  - *Death Ray/Blow Your Mind* virus
  - *Returned Mail* virus
  - *Bud Frogs* virus (possible hoax, but certainly overblown)
- Chain letter flare-ups
  - FCC modem tax alert
  - Internet shutdown day
  - AOL password-stealing virus
  - Mirabilis ICQ virus
  - *Join the Crew* virus
  - *Penpal Greetings* virus

To combat the problem of false alarms about viruses, web pages such as this one, at <http://www. kumite.com/myths>, have become more common on the Internet.

Privacy on the Internet

Privacy on the Internet is becoming an increasingly serious concern to many cybercitizens. Even a short jaunt into cyberspace to read your E-mail, check out a few newsgroups, or browse the Web can compromise your privacy. In an article for *Internet World* magazine, Bill Mann revealed the depth of the problem when he said,

> *Someone is watching you, likely, several someones are—anyone from your boss to a nighttime employee at your Internet service provider, and possibly even someone from the government. From the moment you connect to the Net, you are leaking information to the world about who you are, what you do and what you're interested in. . . . The computers that make up the Net monitor and often record everything you do while online.*[8]

Who's Watching You Surf the Web?

Many programs that are used to run Web sites include log files, which record data about every request for information that a Web site receives. Log files gather information such as the geographic area visitors come from and how often they visit the Web page. They can also tell the Web site operator what type of computer you use, what kind of Web browser you have installed in your computer, which Web page you just came from, and the time and date of your visit.

To enable them to collect even more information, some Webmasters (persons who operate Web sites) have installed cookie features on their Web sites. Cookie stands for "Client-side persistent information." A cookie is a small program that is transferred to your hard disk when you visit a Web site that automatically identifies you every time you return to that Web site.

The primary uses for cookies are to analyze the effectiveness of Web advertising, to track the movements of visitors through a Web site to see which links are read and which are ignored, and to recognize frequent visitors so they don't have to enter identifying information every time they log in. Cookies can also be used to personalize Web pages so Internet users can easily return to their favorite areas on the page without having to go through links that don't interest them.

However, the information provided by log files and cookies, along with other sources of information available through the Internet, could conceivably allow a Web site operator to put together a detailed profile of Web page visitors by tracking their on-line activities. This capability has caused many people to worry about how much of their privacy they compromise by going on the Web.

Going to a Web page that offers an anonymizer program is one popular way to protect your on-line privacy. When you visit an anonymizer site, such as <http://www.anonymizer.com>, you are given an anonymous identity to use while surfing the Web. That way, you can visit any site you want without having to worry about who might be collecting information about your Internet activities and what they might plan to do with it in the future.

Some people in the computer industry feel that concern about cookies has been overstated. Dave McClure, executive director of the Association of Online Professionals said, "If there were a valid threat to privacy or a single documented case of the technology being abused to the detriment of consumers, we might feel differently. But we can't allow vague fears to dictate the technology, the structure, or the growth of the online industry."[9]

Ethics on the Internet

Many problems regarding ethics on the Internet remain to be solved. Meanwhile, here are some tips, compiled by the Computer Ethics Institute in Washington, D.C., for enjoying your time on the Internet without causing harm to others:

- Don't use a computer to harass or harm other people.

- Don't use a computer to steal.

- Don't write or spread computer viruses.

- Don't use a computer to spread gossip, lies, or urban myths.

- Don't interfere with other people's computer work.

- Don't "hack" or snoop around in other people's computer files.

- Don't use other people's computers or software without permission.

- Don't use shareware programs (computer programs that you are allowed to try free for a limited time) for extended periods unless you pay for them.

- Don't claim material you found on the Internet as your own work.

- Don't post articles on newsgroups where they have no relevance.

5

Who Uses the Internet?

Since the mid-1990s, many Americans have been able to enjoy the benefits of being connected to the Internet. A recent survey indicated that about 40 percent of American families now have at least one computer in their home. And many of these computers are connected to the Internet.

The rapid growth of computer and Internet use brings the Information Superhighway into more homes every day. Still, many Americans cannot afford access to this wonderful resource. The 1997 edition of the *World Almanac and*

Book of Facts states that the average World Wide Web user had a household income of $59,000.[1] Many families in the United States have incomes far below that level. Al Weisel writes in *People* magazine, "While the Web is no longer solely the domain of academics and computer geeks, it's not nearly as diverse as the real world. Internet surfers, like the beach variety, are still largely male and white."[2]

So the question is, will the Internet benefit all of society? Or will it further divide the haves and have-nots? Several things are being done to help level the playing field so that more people will have access to the Internet.

Internet in the Library

Public libraries have long been a source of information for people who cannot afford to buy all the books and magazines they would like to read. Now, many libraries are extending their services to make the Internet available to those who cannot afford it. "Today's library is trendy, up-to-date, plugged in, and most definitely not set outside of the ordinary day. . . . You can get movies there and Nintendo games, drink cappuccino and surf cyberspace," writes Sallie Tisdale in an article for *Harper's* magazine.[3]

There are nearly 9,000 public libraries in the United States. As of 1997, nearly half of the nation's libraries had computer stations that connect to the Internet for their patrons to use.

Many libraries now offer Internet access to their patrons.

WebTV

In 1996, a new and less expensive way of accessing the Internet was introduced—WebTV. WebTV Networks, Inc., of Palo Alto, California, hailed their product as "a no-compromise, high-performance solution that provides easy-to-use affordable Internet access wherever there is a television and a standard phone line."[4]

With a WebTV Internet terminal, your television screen can be used to view Web pages, visit and post messages to newsgroups, chat, send E-mail, and listen to Internet audio services. If you own a printer, you can attach it to the WebTV box and print out the Web pages and other materials you view.[5]

Less Expensive Computers

In the mid-1990s, accessing the Internet became more affordable when the price of multimedia computers dropped to the $1,000 to $1,500 range. Only a few years before, similar computers would have cost two to three times that much. But the public demand for affordable machines that can connect to the Internet encouraged several computer manufacturers to lower their prices in the interest of gaining more sales.

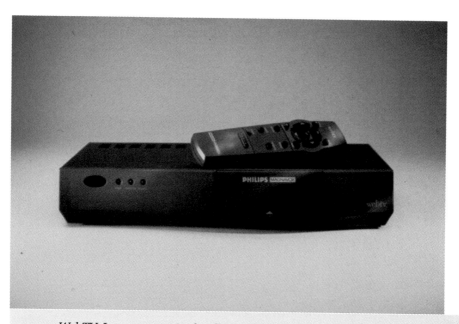

WebTV Internet terminals allow people to access the Internet through their television.

Lower priced computers, such as this model manufactured by Monorail, make it easier for a person on a budget to access the Internet.

A number of computer manufacturers, including Compaq, Omnirail, and Packard Bell, are designing computers especially for this market. While these computers may not have all the power, speed, or hard disk space of their more expensive counterparts, they have opened the benefits of the Internet to many people. Owen Linderholm, a freelance author who has been involved with the computer industry since 1980, says of these budget models, "All in all, most of these PCs are surprisingly acceptable, many with lots of extras."[6]

Freenets

Dozens of communities in the United States have started freenets. These community computer networks, which are run by local organizations, allow people to access community information and at least some parts of the Internet without having to pay an Internet provider. Most freenets are funded jointly by the community, government, and area businesses. Some are set up as telnet services, and others can be viewed with a Web browser. The costs, if any, are usually much lower than what most Internet providers and on-line services charge.

Every community freenet is different. Some only offer a few databases on community and government services. But most freenets host a much wider variety of offerings—including Web browsers, Internet newsgroups, several on-line newspapers, forums, and live chats with other freenet members. These resources have become so popular that people living outside the local area they serve enjoy accessing them through the World Wide Web. Over one hundred freenets have already been set up in the United States. Many more are planned for the near future.

The Blacksburg Electronic Village is a good example of what free or inexpensive Internet service can do for a community. Sixty percent of the residents in this Virginia town of thirty-five thousand make use of the service. Blacksburg residents use the Electronic Village to compare prices at local businesses, do their banking, see which books are available at the library, listen to local bands, express their views to local politicians, browse the World Wide Web, send E-mail to each other, chat on line, and more. Students can even contact their teachers with questions about homework assignments through the community network.

Andrew Cohill, one of the project's directors, said, "We're giving people a new way to communicate with friends, family, neighbors and local business. It's making us a stronger community. We're providing an analogue of the old general store front porch."[7]

A survey taken by *USA Weekend* confirmed Cohill's praise of the computer network. Of 219 people surveyed, 185 believed that the Blacksburg Electronic Village had drawn their community closer together. Only 33 said that the closeness of the community had not been affected, and one said that it had made people in Blacksburg less close.[8]

What Remains to Be Done

Despite all the progress that has been made, there is still much work to be done. Many people who could benefit from the Internet are still not able to use it.

As of early 1997, only 38 percent of K–12 grade schools had any type of Internet connection. And only 10 percent of American K–12 classrooms were able to log on to the World Wide Web. Budget constraints, lack of training, and inadequate wiring head the list of reasons why most of America's

BLACKSBURG
electronic village

Blacksburg, Virginia

Community
Arts
Organizations
Religion
Sports
Education
Library
Museums
Schools
People
Discussion
Seniors
Government
Health
Village Mall
Visitor's Center

Search Tools
Help Desk
▼ Full Index

News

Kevin Powell
Feb. 17, 1998 8PM,
Colonial Hall, Squires
Student Center. The
Black Student Alliance
Of VT Presents.... an
award winning Poet,
Vibe's senior writer, and
former MTV's Real
World cast member
Kevin Powell speaking
about music, politics,
culture, the urban youth,
and his new book
"Keepin' It Real".
231-6076.

**"Making
Winston-Salem a
Virtual Village"**
Virginia town's linkup
sparks our city's creative
juices. *by William
Holmes*.

The CAVE
Tour the CAVE -- a
"virtual reality"
environment in the WPI
Building in the
Corporate Research
Center. Tours are given
every Tuesday and
Thursday 7:30-8:30 am
indefinitely.

**Special Olympics 1998
Regional Basketball
Tournament**
Sunday, February 15, 1998,
Cassell Coliseum.
Individuals interested in
serving on a committee
should attend an
organizational meeting
february 10 at 5:30 pm in
the Donaldson Brown
Center (CEC). 951-2918 or
vasosw@juno.com

Retire Blacksburg '98
June 1998. Register now,
space is limited. 231-5182.

**Downtown Blacksburg
Scavenger Hunt**
Feb 1-Feb 28. Entry forms
are in participating
merchants' stores. Three age
groups: under 12, 13-20, and
21 and over. Prizes to a
winner in each age group.

[Old Messages || **POST** a Message
]

Weather Underground Forecast
Blacksburg National Weather
Service

About the BEV | **Services** | **Training** | **Research** |
Starting a Village

*On-line communities, such as the Blacksburg Electronic
Village at <http://www.bev.net>, which serves the town of
Blacksburg, Virginia, create a new medium for people to read
local news or for businesses to advertise their products.*

schools are not yet part of the Information Superhighway.

In an article written for *Discover* magazine, Vice-President Al Gore said,

> *The president and I believe strongly that every classroom, library, hospital, and clinic in the United States must be connected to the National Information Infrastructure by the end of the century. As a nation, we cannot tolerate—nor in the long run can we afford—a society in which some children become fully educated and others do not, in which some patients benefit from shared medical expertise and others do not, in which some people have access to lifetime learning and job training and others do not.*[9]

Fortunately, programs sponsored by government, business, and private organizations are currently under way that will help solve the problem. Here are a few examples of what is currently being done:

- In May 1997, the Federal Communications Commission approved a $10 billion plan to help wire schools and libraries that could not otherwise afford the Internet. The plan, which gives discounts of 20 to 90 percent, will bring the Internet to nearly 50 million children who otherwise would not have access to it.

- The national Net Day program encourages volunteers to go to schools and wire them for the Internet. President Clinton hailed the program as "an exciting response [to his challenge] to connect every classroom and library in America to the Information Superhighway by the year 2000."[10]

- Challenge Grants for Technology in Education is a United States government program that will help put computers into more schools. The 1997 federal budget included nearly $57 million for this program. That is a 50 percent increase over the program's funding in the 1996 budget.

- Millions of dollars of profits from Bill Gates's book *The Road Ahead* are being donated to help bring the Internet into schools and libraries across the nation that could not otherwise afford it.

- AT&T's Learning Network has made a $150 million five-year commitment to help more schools get on the Internet. This program includes grants, an on-line training program for teachers, and discounts on AT&T's WorldNet Internet connections.

6

How Large Can the Internet Grow?

The Internet is growing at an astounding rate. As of late 1996, the population of the Internet was approximately 40 million people. That is more than twice the number of people who were connected to the worldwide communications system a year earlier. And every thirty seconds, twenty more people are logging on to the Internet for the first time.[1]

The amount of E-mail that passes through the Internet is another way of measuring just how fast the Internet is growing. In 1994, 776 billion pieces of E-mail passed through American-based computer networks. Experts predict that in 1997, that number will have risen to 2.6 trillion. By the year 2000, the Internet will likely be called upon to deliver an astounding 6.6 trillion pieces of E-mail.[2]

Increased Traffic Causes Problems

While Internet access and use has been encouraged by the government, educators, the business community, and Internet providers, the dramatic rise in people wanting access to the Internet is starting to cause problems. Every piece of E-mail, every Web page that someone wants to download, and every newsgroup that a Net citizen reads must be processed by the Internet's computers and circuitry to reach its destination.

The Internet can be very congested during peak usage hours. Mark Fedor, director of engineering at PSINet, Inc., in Herndon, Virginia, said, "Sending data through a router is almost like filling up a bucket. When it gets filled up, a bunch of data spills over the top. When the Internet is congested, overloaded routers actually throw away some packets."[3] Most systems are designed to scan for this problem and retransmit any data that were lost. Still, the overload causes a delay that Internet users must endure while the missing information is being recovered.

Already, there have been signs of what might happen if the data overload continues. In 1996, several major Internet services, including America Online, MCI, Netcom On-Line, and AT&T WorldNet experienced system shutdowns that prevented their customers from using the Internet service for periods lasting from hours to days.[4]

Bulk E-mail Advertising

In recent years, a number of companies have gone into the business of bulk mailing advertisements to Internet users via E-mail. Many such ads promote fraudulent get-rich-quick schemes. Others are advertisements for legitimate products and services, such as computers, modems, and Internet services.

To many Internet users, these bulk E-mailed advertisements are equivalent to unwanted junk mail. It is an annoyance to have to delete them. And it is time-consuming to sort through the bunch to find the messages they really want to read. When millions of such messages are sent over the Internet on a daily basis, it contributes significantly to slowing down the entire Internet system.

Experts are trying to solve this problem. One idea is to allow people who do not want to receive such postings to register their preference. Keeping a record of who does not want unsolicited E-mail advertising would benefit everyone. Advertisers would be spared the expense of sending advertisements to people who are not interested in them. It would save time for people who do not want to read or sort through unwanted mail. And the Internet system itself would be spared the burden of transmitting unwanted messages. Prodigy, America Online, and a few other Internet services are already

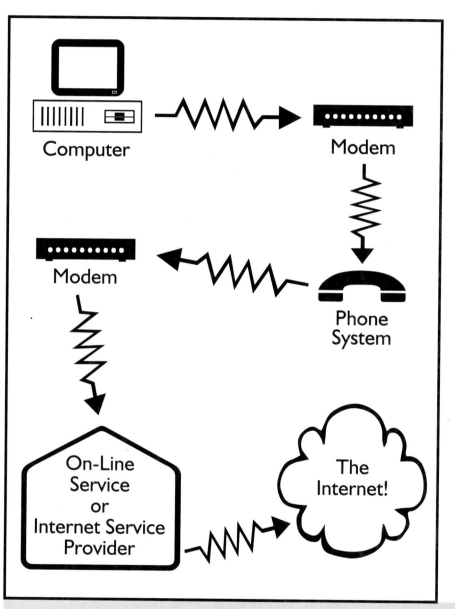

This diagram shows how your computer connects to the Internet.

trying this approach. Unfortunately, few bulk E-mail advertisers have gone to the trouble of requesting a copy of these preference lists.

Some Internet service providers and on-line services have recently added a clause to their service contracts that forbids subscribers from sending out bulk E-mail advertisements. In 1997, Earthlink, an Internet service provider based in Pasadena, California, fined one of its members $200 for sending out unsolicited bulk E-mail through their service. But with the kind of profit that can sometimes be made through bulk E-mail advertising, it will likely take much more than this to significantly slow the flow of unwanted Internet advertisements.[5]

Unlimited Access

When Internet providers and on-line services started offering unlimited access for a set monthly fee in the mid-1990s, use of the Internet increased dramatically. No longer did subscribers have to watch the clock or worry about how high their bill might be.

At first, only companies that provided direct Internet service offered unlimited access. But soon, on-line services, such as America Online and Prodigy, decided to offer unlimited service at a competitive price to hold on to their customers.

The new unlimited access plan dramatically changed the way that many people used the Internet. People who once signed on to the Internet just long enough to check their E-mail messages or perhaps check out a few newsgroups or Web sites now started to spend much more time logged on to the Net. Some Internet service subscribers gathered in chat rooms, exchanging electronic messages with anyone who happened to be on-line at the time. Others browsed the Web for hours, moving casually from one link to another. Still others left their computers hooked up to the Internet while they watched TV, talked to friends, or went about other activities—just in case they thought of something they wanted to do on the Internet later on.

While unlimited service plans gained instant popularity with Internet users, this dramatic increase in traffic soon started to slow down the entire Internet system. Web pages took longer to download. Internet games did not run as fast as they once did. Sometimes, Internet search engines were so congested that they did not work at all.

When America Online, the nation's largest on-line service, first offered its unlimited access pricing plan to its members in December 1996, it received a much larger response than expected. Members often encountered busy phone lines when they tried to dial into the service. Sometimes, they could not access their E-mail for hours because of the logjam. And once they were able to get through, many discovered that the E-mail system, Web browser, and other popular features ran much more slowly than usual.

New Applications Require More Memory

The type of material that is transmitted through the Internet has also changed. In the early 1990s,

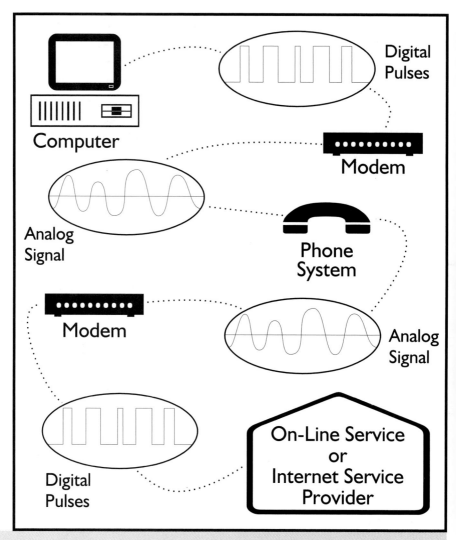

Digital Pulses

Computer

Modem

Analog Signal

Phone System

Modem

Analog Signal

Digital Pulses

On-Line Service or Internet Service Provider

Modems allow computers to communicate with each other. They translate the digital transmissions of a computer into analog waves that can pass through telephone lines, just as your voice does. If the modem speaker is turned on when you dial into an Internet service, you can hear the analog signal as a series of sounds.

E-mail messages and plain text documents made up the bulk of material transmitted through the Internet. Only occasionally would someone download larger pieces of data—such as a picture or a computer program. This was, in part, because of slow modem speeds and the high cost of connection time. But all that has changed. Many of the newer Internet applications require the transfer of tremendous amounts of data from one point to another.

Since the mid-1990s, Web browsing has become one of the more popular activities on the Internet. Use of the World Wide Web rises about 300 percent a year. In addition to text, Web pages often contain professional-quality graphics, audio files, and other multimedia applications. These take up much more space than plain text transmissions.

Another new application is videoconferencing— sending live video of business meetings and other events across the Internet. When videoconferencing was first introduced, the pictures were very choppy. Because of the relatively slow modem speeds at the time, a new image could only be transmitted every several seconds. Advancements in computer technology in the mid-1990s, however, have greatly improved the quality of videoconferencing. Businesses that use videoconferencing services install special lines that carry more data than traditional telephone lines. Most live video transmissions that pass through the Internet still do not compare with the quality of television. But faster computer speeds and speedier modems have done a great deal to improve the picture quality.

Yet massive amounts of data must be transmitted for video or sound transmissions. As this type of service becomes more popular, it will undoubtedly tax the limited resources of the Internet's lines and servers.

Internet expert Edmund X. De Jesus said,

> *The basic problem has to do with the large numbers of packets necessary to send sound and picture files. If someone is watching a movie or listening to sound, that requires hundreds of packets [of data] per minute. And if many people are doing these things, the total number of packets being sent increases in multiples. It's just like a major highway. The more people using the road, the slower the getting on, getting there, and getting off gets. The Internet is approaching rush hour.*[6]

How Much Traffic Can the Internet Bear?

The increasingly heavy load of data being sent through the Internet has caused some computer experts to become concerned. Just how much traffic can the system handle?

So far, only small portions of the Internet have been brought to a halt by overcrowding and other problems. This is because the Internet is not one computer network but a combination of thousands of individual networks that can transmit data through many different paths.

In an article for *The Net* magazine, computer writer Jon Phillips said,

When you hear someone say "The Net was down today," you know you're listening to a neophyte [newcomer] or an old-timer who's casually referring to his connection to the Internet. In fact, the Internet's most significant quality is that it's not a single network, but an aggregate [mixture] of many different networks, all tied together by cooperating routers. The system can be likened [compared] to an infrastructure of slow-speed dirt roads, medium-speed city streets, and high-speed cross-country turnpikes.[7]

No one knows exactly how much traffic the Internet's networks and routers can hold before the entire system shuts down or becomes too crowded for people to use. But the increasing load of data traffic on the Internet brings us closer to that crisis every day. Douglas E. Comer, professor of computer science at Purdue University, said, "At various times, people have predicted the imminent collapse of the Internet. A few years ago, for example, some predicted that the Internet could not survive past March of 1993. The predictions of doom have been incorrect. Each time the traffic has approached the capacity of a backbone network, a new backbone of technology has been found with significantly more capacity."[8]

Who Should Maintain the Internet?

There are things that can be done to help prevent the Internet from suffering a serious collapse. Adding more routers, servers, modems, and other equipment to help carry the heavy load of traffic is part of the answer. Additional telephone lines to move the traffic must also be installed as soon as possible.

"It's not a question of whether the Internet needs funding; it's a question of who's going to pay it, how the money is going to be divided, how much is going to change hands, and how often. A $19.95 monthly Internet access fee is barely paying for the resources you consume on a local level. Only a tiny part of it feeds the needs of the infrastructure," said Joel Snyder, a senior partner at Opus One, an Internet provider and consulting service in Tucson, Arizona.[9]

Who Should Pay?

Since the Internet benefits the general public, some people believe the government should bear part of the responsibility for expanding the Internet's computer systems enough to provide access for all who want to use it.

Other people feel that financing the Internet's expansion should be left to the private sector. The business community is benefiting greatly from people having access to the Internet. Most medium- to large-sized companies depend on the Internet for their everyday communications needs. They also use it to do market research and to reach potential customers.

How do you think the expansion of the Internet should be financed? Should those who use the Internet pay for the additional routers, servers, and other equipment required to keep the Internet in service? Should the government appropriate more tax money to help solve the problem? Should the business community have to pay more? Or should a combination of these approaches be used? These are the questions that must be answered to ensure that the Internet continues to operate as it should.

7

The Future of the Internet

"It is still very early. . . .We are still in the middle ages of computers," says Michael Dertouzos, head of Massachusetts Institute of Technology's (MIT) Laboratory for Computer Science.[1]

In the past decade, the Internet has come a long way. It has gone from being a complex tool of computer experts and scientists to an exciting new communications medium that even small children can access with ease. Most of the applications that are commonly used on the Net today did not even exist when the Internet was created. Considering that, it is hard for anyone to guess what the Internet might become in the future.

Whatever the Internet becomes, one thing is certain: Much of its development will involve blending and improving existing communications systems. In a speech titled "The Information Superhighway—An On Ramp for Students," FCC Commissioner Rachelle Chong explained how many technologies that are currently in use will eventually merge to create new and better services.

> *Visionaries generally describe the future to be a multimedia world of seamless, two-way video, voice and data connections that will allow people to communicate on a new, more advanced level, including interactivity. Thus, current technologies will be merged into what is expected to become an extraordinary whole. This so-called convergence of formerly diverse industries will become the driving force behind the Info Superhighway.[2]*

High-Speed Internet Access

For all of this to take place, high-speed Internet access is essential. Today's computers and modems are able to process data at speeds that were unthought of several years ago. However, one thing is holding back the development of high-quality video on the Internet. And that is the outdated telephone lines that carry Internet data to and from most homes, schools, and businesses. Dr. Scott R. Becker, owner of the Becker Internet Group Internet service in Kiowa, Kansas, said, "Unfortunately, the bandwidth [capacity to carry data] you need for good video just isn't there. No matter what kind of modem you have, the best we can do over the standard telephone lines is to send a 1-1/2 inch picture at the rate of 2 to 3 frames per second. And that looks very choppy compared with the 30 frames per second you have with standard television."[3]

At present, most home computer users access the Internet at speeds of 33,600 bits per second or less. Modems designed to carry 56,000 bits per second are available. But at this time, few ISPs (Internet Service Providers) or on-line services are equipped to provide their customers with that service.

ISDN Lines

Many businesses, schools, libraries, and other institutions—as well as some home computer users who can afford it—have upgraded from a traditional phone line to an ISDN (Integrated Services Digital Network) line. ISDN lines, which are specially designed to carry digital data, allow you to access the Internet at speeds of up to 128,000 bits per second—nearly four times as fast as the computer modems that are currently in use.

Cable Modems

Cable television companies in some areas are starting to offer high-speed Internet service. With a cable modem, it is possible to access the Internet at 10 million bits per second and receive video signals of the same quality as cable television signals.

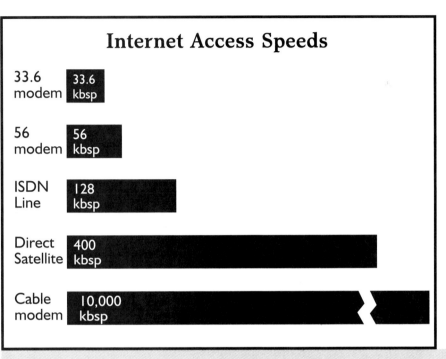

Internet Access Speeds

- 33.6 modem — 33.6 kbsp
- 56 modem — 56 kbsp
- ISDN Line — 128 kbsp
- Direct Satellite — 400 kbsp
- Cable modem — 10,000 kbsp

This illustration shows the differences in Internet access speeds through modems, cable modems, ISDN lines, and via satellite.

Currently, only 2 to 3 percent of Americans have access to a cable modem service.[4] *Computer Life* writer William O'Neal said, "Some hardware manufacturers, including Bay Networks, Hewlett-Packard, and Motorola, have already begun producing cable modems. But it could be years—even decades—before the technology ends up in most of our homes. [At this time] most cable providers are far from ready for two-way communications."[5]

The Internet via Satellite

While some Internet enthusiasts look to ISDN lines and cable modems for faster Internet service in the future, others believe that satellites hold the key to high-speed Internet access.

Hughes Network Systems' satellite Internet service, DirecPC, allows subscribers to connect to the Web at speeds of 400,000 bits per second. People who use satellite services to access the Internet still must use a traditional modem for sending and receiving E-mail, transferring files, reading newsgroups, and using Internet services other than the World Wide Web.

Plans are already in the works to dramatically expand satellite Internet service. Teledesic Corporation, along with Boeing Co., hopes to launch 288 low-earth-orbiting satellites within the next several years to provide high-speed Internet access. With that many satellites in service, they plan to offer all of the Internet through satellite, not just the World Wide Web. (Updates about the project can be found at <http://www.teledesic.com>.)

However, some experts doubt that the ambitious undertaking will ever get off the ground. As of the late 1990s, only fifty satellites are being launched from Earth a year. Even if the expenses for putting that many satellites into orbit can be met, it will be difficult to find launch facilities for that many rockets. Daniel Hastings, professor of space systems and space propulsion at MIT, said, "It's not just unprecedented for a private company to launch 288 satellites in a year, it's unprecedented period."[6]

Despite the difficulties with putting the Teledesic program into service, Hastings believes that in the long run satellites are the only practical way to insure worldwide, high-speed access to the Internet. In an interview for *Netguide* magazine, he said, "A satellite system, once in orbit, gives you an instant global infrastructure. By comparison, the cost of laying terrestrial fiber-optic cable everywhere in the world is too high to even conceive of."[7]

Whatever direction the development of high-speed Internet access takes, one thing is certain. The ability of Internet subscribers to quickly download large amounts of data will open the door to many new kinds of entertainment and information presentations.

Will the Internet Become More Like Television?

As the Internet becomes faster, easier to access, and less expensive, some people fear that it will become more and more like the corporate-controlled mediums of television, newspapers, and magazines.

Products that make it possible to access the Internet through a television have undoubtedly allowed many people who could not afford to buy a computer to log on to the World Wide Web and other parts of cyberspace. But some experts question whether the majority of people who buy this type of service will want to fully participate in the forums, newsgroups, and other interactive parts of the Internet. Instead, they fear that many in this new group of Internet users will become "Web-watchers" who use the World Wide Web merely as a new group of television stations they can view. Media critic Mark Kingwell warned, "The troubling thing is that, under cover of the allegedly democratic cover of wider access, the revolutionary interactive possibilities of a democratic medium are gradually being allowed to slip away. Television isn't expanding into the Net; it's shrinking the Net to fit the cramped dimensions of the box."[8]

Some people also fear that push technology services, which were first introduced to the public in

Whatever the future brings, books are still a useful way to learn about the Internet.

February 1996 when the PointCast Network was launched, are another step in that direction. Push technology allows Internet subscribers to select the kind of material they want to view by specifying channels, such as CNN Weather, ESPN Sports Wire, Business Wire, and so forth.

But while news services that use push technology can be a time-saver for busy people who do not want to take the time to search the Web for information, they also have their drawbacks. The news and other information provided by push services are limited by the offerings of the channels subscribers select. In effect, by using a push service, you are giving control over what you view to the corporate media.

The Internet in the Twenty-First Century

While no one can accurately predict what the Internet will become—or the changes it will bring to our lives in the future—many experts are optimistic.

Bill Gates, the owner and founder of the Microsoft software company said in his book *The Road Ahead,*

> *Despite the problems posed by the information highway, my enthusiasm for it remains boundless. . . . We are watching something historic happen, and it will affect the world seismatically, rocking us in the same way that the discovery of the scientific method, the invention of printing, and the arrival of the Industrial Age did. . . . Above all, and in countless new ways, the information highway will give us choices that can put us in touch with entertainment, information, and each other.*[9]

Guide to Internet Newsgroups

The names of Internet newsgroups are divided into two or more parts. The first part of a newsgroup name identifies the general category of information that an Internet user can expect to find in it. Here are a few examples:

ALT—Alternative

BIZ—Business

COMP—Computer related

K12—Education

MISC—Miscellaneous

REC—Recreation

SCI—Science

SOC—Social

•••••••••••••

The second part of the newsgroup name tells even more about the kind of information that can be found there. To better define the type of information they contain, many newsgroups have three- or even four-part names. Some examples of newsgroup names are alt.censorship

alt.journalism

alt.radio.pirate

rec.arts.startrek.current

rec.music.rem

rec.pets.cats

rec.radio.shortwave

rec.travel.air

sci.space.shuttle

Before posting on a newsgroup, it is a good idea to read messages for a while and become familiar with it. Often, there is a FAQ page that will provide answers to Frequently Asked Questions. Also, you should be careful to only post messages that are relevant to the subject the newsgroup covers.

Organizations to Contact

Center for Civic Networking
P.O. Box 65272
Washington, DC 20037
Phone (202) 362-3831
E-mail: ccn@civicnet.org
<http://www.civicnet.org>

Center for Democracy and Technology
1001 G St. NW, Suite 700 E
Washington, DC 20001
Phone (202) 637-9800
E-mail: info@cdt.org
<http://www.cdt.org>

Coalition for Networked Information
21 Dupont Circle
Washington, DC 20036
Phone (202) 296-5098
E-mail: joan@cni.org
<http://www.cni.org>

Electronic Frontier Foundation
P.O. Box 170190
San Francisco, CA 94117
Phone (415) 668-7171
E-mail: eff@eff.org
<http:// www.eff.org>

Electronic Privacy Information Center
666 Pennsylvania Ave. SE, Suite 301
Washington, DC 20003
Phone (202) 544-9240
E-mail: info@epic.org
<http://www.epic.org>

Institute for Global Communications
P.O. Box 29904
San Francisco, CA 94129-0904
Phone (415) 561-6100
E-mail: support@igc.apc.org
<http://www.igc.org/igc>

Interactive Services Association
8403 Colesville Rd, Suite 865
Silver Spring, MD 20910
Phone (301) 495-4955
E-mail: isa@aol.com
<http://www.isa.net>

Internet Society
12020 Sunrise Valley Drive, Suite 210
Reston, VA 20191-3429
Phone (703) 648-9888 or
(USA only) 800-468-9507
E-mail: membership@isoc.org
<http://www.isoc.org>

Organization for Community Networks
P.O. Box 32175
Euclid, OH 44132
Phone (216) 731-9801
E-mail: jmk@ofcn.org
<http://ofcn.org>

World Wide Web Consortium
Massachusetts Institute of Technology
Laboratory for Computer Science
545 Technology Square
Cambridge, MA 02139
Phone (617) 253-2613
E-mail: admin@w3.org
<http://www.w3.org>

The Development
of the Internet

1969—ARPANET (Advanced Research Projects Agency Network) is commissioned by the U.S. Department of Defense. It links computers at UCLA, the University of California at Santa Barbara, the University of Utah, and Stanford Research Institute.

1973—ARPANET makes its first international connections to University College of London and the Royal Radar Establishment of Norway.

1981—BITNET (Because It's Time Network) is established.

1986—NSFNET (National Science Foundation Network) links five supercomputers to aid in scientific research.

1986—Cleveland Freenet is established as the first free local computer network.

1988—Robert Tappan Morris releases his "worm" program into the Internet, disabling thousands of computers.

1990—Electronic Frontier Foundation (EFF) is founded.

1991—The World Wide Web (WWW) is introduced.

1991—The controversial encryption program Pretty Good Privacy (PGP) is released.

1992—The Internet Society is chartered.

1993—President Bill Clinton becomes the first president to use E-mail, and the White House puts up its own Web page: <http://www.whitehouse.gov>.

1993—Businesses and the media begin to take notice of the Internet.

1995—Commercial on-line services, such as CompuServe, America Online, and Prodigy, start to provide full Internet access.

1995—Real Audio allows people to listen to radio stations and other real-time audio transmissions over the Internet.

1996—WebTV makes it possible for many people who cannot afford a computer to access the Internet.

Chapter Notes

Chapter 1. The Exciting World of the Internet

1. Staff writers, "24 Hours in Cyberspace," *U.S. News & World Report*, October 21, 1996, p. 73.

2. Steven Boggess, "Odyssey in Egypt Middle School Students Dig Ancient Egypt via the Internet," n.d., <http://www.website1.com/odyssey/summary.html> (1997).

3. Staff writers, ibid.

4. Linda J. Engelman, "Good Vibrations," *Internet World*, May 1996, p. 118.

5. Jeff Ubois, "Future Effect," *Internet World*, December 1996, p. 78.

6. Paul Gilster, *The New Internet Navigator* (New York: John Wiley & Sons, 1995), p. 275.

7. Ibid., p. 276.

**Chapter 2. How the Internet Is
Changing Our Lives**

1. Andrea Stone, "Life Begins to Compute," *USA Today*, February 14, 1996, p. 2A.

2. Joe Panepinto, "The Year of the Web," n.d., <http://www.zdnet.com/familypc> (March 1997).

3. Betsey Wagner et al., "Where Computers Do Work," *U.S. News & World Report*, December 2, 1996, p. 93.

4. Maria Newman, "College Courses at Your Convenience on the Internet," n.d., <http://www.nytimes.com> (November 3, 1996).

5. Stone, ibid.

6. James H. Snider, "The Information Superhighway as Environmental Menace," *The Futurist*, March/April 1995 reprinted in Charles P. Cozic, ed., *The Information Highway* (San Diego: Greenhaven Press, 1996), p. 137.

7. Steve Rimmer, *Planet Internet* (New York: Windcrest/McGraw-Hill, 1995), p. 22.

8. Douglas E. Comer, *The Internet Book* (Englewood Cliffs, N.J.: Prentice Hall, 1994), p. 253.

9. Leslie Miller, "Online World Creates New Parental Concerns," n.d., <http://www. USAToday.com> (March 19, 1997).

10. Electric Minds Web page n.d., <http://www. minds.com> (October 30, 1997).

11. David Shenk, *Data Smog: Surviving the Information Glut* (San Francisco: HarperEdge, 1997), p. 113.

12. Miller, ibid.

13. Cornelia Grumman, Chicago Tribune staff writer, "http://www.HELP!" n.d., <http://www. ChicagoTribune.com> (June 26, 1996).

Chapter 3. Who Controls the Internet?

1. Laurrel Merlindo, "Postcards from the Internet," *Computer Life*, April 1997, p. 55.

2. Margaret Mannix, "Have I got a deal for you!" *U.S. News & World Report*, October 27, 1997, p. 59.

3. David W. Chen, "Attacking and Defending the Internet Yet Again," *The New York Times*, October 3, 1997.

4. Mannix, ibid.

5. Ibid.

6. David Leonhardt, "Hey Kid, Buy This!" *Business Week*, June 30, 1997, p. 67.

7. Larry Armstrong, "Pssst! Come into My Web," *Business Week*, June 30, 1997, p. 67.

8. Gus Venditto, "Safe Computing," *Internet World*, September 1996, p. 49.

9. Randall E. Stross, "The Cyber Vice Squad," *U.S. News & World Report*, March 17, 1997 p. 45.

10. Abraham Cooper, "Perspective on Hate on the Internet" n.d., <http://www.weisenthal.com> (1995).

11. Ibid.

12. Steven Levy, "Blaming the Web," *Newsweek*, April 7, 1997, p. 46.

13. Joshua Quittner, "Life and Death on the Web," *Time*, April 7, 1997, p. 47.

14. (no author given) Abridged from the National Coalition for the Protection of Children and Families brochure, *Children, Pornography, and Cyberspace: The Problem, Solutions, and the Current Congressional Debate*, October 1995, reprinted in Charles P. Cozic, ed., *The Information Highway* (San Diego: Greenhaven Press, 1996), pp. 159–160.

15. Pamela Mendels, "Worldwide, Internet Restrictions Are Growing," n.d. <http://www.nytimes.com> (September 10, 1996).

16. Gene Mesher, "The Internet in Asia," *Internet World*, December 1996, p. 57.

17. Mendels, ibid.

18. Channel A staff, n.d., <http://www.chA.com> (October 2, 1996).

19. James Exon, *Washington Times*, April 16, 1995, reproduced in Charles P. Cozic, ed., *The Information Highway* (San Diego: Greenhaven Press, 1996), p. 158.

20. Andrew Kantor, "CDA Overturned, but Other Legislation Looms," *Internet World*, September 1996, p. 16.

21. (no author or date given) Net Nanny Ltd. Corporate Backgrounder.

22. Langdon Winner, "Electronically Implanted Values," *Technology Review*, February/March 1997, p. 69.

23. Jon Katz, "The Rights of Kids in the Digital Age," *Wired*, July 1996, pp. 168–170.

Chapter 4. Security on the Internet

1. John McAffe and Colin Haynes, *Computer Viruses, Worms, Data Diddlers, Killer Programs, and Other Threats to Your System* (New York: St. Martin's Press, 1989), p. 7.

2. Karen Judson, *Computer Crime: Phreaks, Spies, and Salami Slicers* (Springfield, N.J.: Enslow Publishers, Inc., 1994), p. 6.

3. Garry S. Howard, *Introduction to Internet Security: From Basics to Beyond* (Rocklin, Calif.: Prima Publishing, 1995), pp. 249–250.

4. Edmund L. Andrews, "U.S. Restrictions Give European Encryption a Boost," n.d., <http://www.nytimes.com> (April 7, 1997).

5. Jim Cope, "Guarding Data," *PC Today*, April 1996, p. 57.

6. Kenneth R. van Wyk, "Macros Under the Microscope," *Infosecurity News*, January/February 1997, p. 34.

7. Ellen Grant, "This Is Not a Joke" *Info Security Magazine*, October 1997, pp. 54–55.

8. Bill Mann, "Stopping You Watching Me," *Internet World*, April 1997, p. 42.

9. Gary Welz, "Cookie Fears Half-Baked, Says AOP," *Internet World*, August 1997, p. 22.

Chapter 5. Who Uses the Internet?

1. Robert Famighetti, *The World Almanac and Book of Facts 1997* (Mahwah, N.J.: World Almanac Books, 1997), p. 207.

2. Al Weisel, "Plugged In," *People*, June 1997, p. 118.

3. Sallie Tisdale, "Silence, Please," *Harper's*, March 1997, p. 66.

4. Mark Kingwell, "WebTV Unplugged," *Utne Reader*, May–June 1997, pp. 91–92.

5. Ibid., p. 93.

6. Owen Linderholm, "7 PCs Under $1,000," n.d., <http://zeppo.cnet.com/content/reviews> (April 30, 1997).

7. David Diamond, "This Town Is Wired," *USA Weekend*, February 23–25, 1996, p. 4.

8. Ibid., p. 5.

9. Al Gore, "Technology Democracy," n.d., <http://www.enews.com/magazines/discover> (October 1994).

10. Bill Clinton, Net Day Press Kit, n.d., <http:/www.netday.org> (1997).

Chapter 6. How Large Can the Internet Grow?

1. John Simons, "Waiting to Download," *U.S. News and World Report*, January 6, 1997, p. 60.

2. S.C. Gwynne and John F. Dickerson, "Lost in the E-mail," *Time*, April 21, 1997, p. 89.

3. Kate Gerwig, "The Lowdown on Internet 'Breakdowns,'" *Netguide*, April 1997, p. 34.

4. Simons, ibid.

5. Margaret Mannix, "Have I got a deal for you!" *U.S. News and World Report*, October 27, 1997, p. 60.

6. Dennis O'Flaherty, "Communications Breakdown," *Internet World*, October 1996, p. 48.

7. Jon Phillips, "How Your Data Snakes Across the Internet," *The Net*, September 1996, p. 45.

8. Douglas Comer, *The Internet* (Englewood Cliffs, N.J.: Prentice Hall, 1995), p. 71.

9. Joel Snyder, "Bits and Bucks," *Internet World*, October 1996, p. 106.

Chapter 7. The Future of the Internet

1. Andrea Stone, "Life Begins to Compute," *USA Today*, February 14, 1996, p. 2A.

2. Rachelle Chong, December 23, 1996, <http://www.fcc.gov/chonglog.html> (1997).

3. Dr. Scott R. Becker, personal interview, May 16, 1997.

4. Ibid.

5. William O'Neal, "Download Derby," *Computer Life*, July 1997, p. 96.

6. Matthew Friedman, "Teledesic: Science Fiction or Reality?" *Netguide*, August 1997, p. 25.

7. Ibid., p. 24.

8. Mark Kingwell, "WebTV Unplugged," *Utne Reader*, May–June 1997, p. 93.

9. Bill Gates, *The Road Ahead* (New York: Viking Penguin, 1995), pp. 272–274.

Glossary

bandwidth—The amount of data that can pass through wires, cable, or other equipment in one second.

BBS—Abbreviation for bulletin-board service.

browser—A software tool used to view Internet resources.

chat room—An Internet site where people can communicate with each other in real time.

cracker—Someone who breaks into computer systems for malicious reasons.

cyberspace—The on-line culture that the Internet has created.

database—A collection of data, such as text files, available on the Internet.

download—To transfer data files from the Internet to your computer.

E-mail—Electronic mail.

FAQ (frequently asked questions)—Most-requested information about a newsgroup or other Internet site or about some other topic.

FTP (File Transfer Protocol)—Format for transferring data from a host computer to a remote computer.

Gopher—A menu-based tool for locating and retrieving information on the Internet.

hacker—Someone who breaks into computer systems that do not belong to them.

home page—The beginning page on a Web site.

HTTP (Hypertext Transfer Protocol)—Format for transferring data between computers on the World Wide Web. Hypertext organizes information by providing links (hyperlinks) to related information.

Internet service provider (ISP)—A company that provides Internet service to residential, educational, or business customers.

modem (modulator-demodulator)—A device used to transmit computer data across telephone lines.

Net citizen or Netizen—A person who is a member of the Internet community.

newbie—A person who is new to the Internet.

newsgroup (Usenet)—An area of the Internet, similar to a bulletin board, where you can post messages for others to read.

password—Word used to confirm your identity.

search engine—A program that searches the Internet for data you request. It counts the number of times a specified word or phrase (query) appears in a document and compiles a list of sites based on that word count.

spam—To send bulk messages indiscriminately to individuals or newsgroups.

telecommuting—To work at home via the Internet, instead of in the office.

teleconference—A conference held over the Internet.

Telnet—A system that allows users in a remote location to run programs on a computer as if they were present.

WWW or Web—Abbreviation for World Wide Web (WWW), an area of the Internet that presents documents containing text, graphics, sound, and even video files.

Further Reading

Books

Banks, Michael A. *Web Psychos, Stalkers, and Pranksters: How to Protect Yourself Online.* Albany, N.Y.: Coriolis Group Books, 1997.

Comer, Douglas E. *The Internet Book: Everything You Need to Know About Computer Networking and How the Internet Works.* Englewood Cliffs, N.J.: Prentice Hall, 1995.

Cozic, Charles P. (ed.) *The Information Highway* (Current Controversies Series). San Diego, Calif.: Greenhaven Press, Inc., 1996.

Eager, Bill. *The Information Superhighway Illustrated: The Full-Color Guide to How It All Works.* Indianapolis, Ind.: Que, 1994.

Gilster, Paul. *The New Internet Navigator.* New York: John Wiley & Sons, Inc., 1995.

Goodman, Danny. *Living at Light Speed: Your Survival Guide to Life on the Information Superhighway.* New York: Random House, 1994.

Howard, Gerry S. *Introduction to Internet Security: From Basics to Beyond.* Rocklin, Calif.: Prima Publishing, 1995.

Judson, Karen. *Computer Crime: Phreaks, Spies, and Salami Slicers.* Springfield, N.J.: Enslow Publishers, Inc., 1994.

Rheingold, Howard. *The Virtual Community: Homesteading on the Electronic Frontier*. Redding, Mass.: Addison-Wesley Publishing Company, 1993.

On the Internet

Classroom Connect: Internet made easy for the classroom <http://www.classroom.com>.

Cyber Angels: a place to learn about Internet safety and security problems <http://www.cyberangels.org>.

Cyberholics Netformation SuperSite <http://www.cyberholics.com>.

Electronic Frontier Foundation's Guide to the Internet <http://www.eff.org/papers/eegti>.

History of the Internet (from the Internet Society) <http://www.isoc.org/internet-history>.

Information on computer-related careers <http://www.microsoft.com/skills2000>.

Internet Traffic Report: monitors the flow of data on the internet around the world <http://www.internettrafficreport.com>.

Netizens: On the History and Impact of the Net <http://www.columbia.edu/~hauben/netbook>.

Index

A
Allison, David, 24
American Civil Liberties
   Union, 52–53
ARPANET, 18–19

B
Becker, Scott R., 103–104
BITNET, 20–21
Blacksburg Electronic
   Village, 85–86, 87
Brooke, Tal, 50
bulletin boards, 20
Burns, Conrad, 29–30

C
cable modems, 104–105
chat rooms, 34, 48
Chong, Rachelle, 54, 55,
   103
Clinton, Bill, 88
Cohill, Andrew, 86
cookies, 76–78
Cooper, Abraham, 49
Communications Decency
   Act, 54–57
Computer Ethics Institute,
   78–79
Consumer Federation of
   America, 46–47
cracker, 64

D
De Jesus, Edmund X., 98
Dingus, Wendell, 69
Doyle, James, 44

E
E-mail advertising, 92, 94
Electric Minds, 35–36
encryption, 67–68
Engelman, Linda J., 9

F
Federal Communications
   Commission, 53–54,
   88
Fedor, Mark, 91
firewalls, 66–67
freenets, 85–86

G
Gates, Bill, 89, 109
Gore, Al, 88

H
hackers, 63–64
Heaven's Gate, 49–50
Human Rights Watch,
   52

I
Internet Fraud Watch, 42
Internet Multicasting
   Service, 32
Internet2, 27, 29
ISDN lines, 104, 105

J
Java, 13

K
Katz, Jon, 60–61
Kingwell, Mark, 108

L

Leonhardt, David, 46
Library of Congress, 10, 11

M

macro viruses, 71–72
Mann, Bill, 76
Manzi, Samuel, 43
McCurdy-Hill, Yvonne, 50
Morris, Robert Tappan, 64–65

N

National Aeronautics and Space Administration, 13, 16, 17, 26
National Coalition for the Protection of Children and Families, 51
National Computer Security Association, 69
Net Day, 88
Net Nanny, 58, 59
Newman, Maria, 27
newsgroups, 9, 22, 110–111
NSFNET, 21

O

Odyssey In Egypt, 5–7

P

passwords, 66
Phillips, Jon, 98–99
PointCast Network, 108–109
Popkes, Daryl, 30
pornography, 43, 47–48, 56, 61–62
Primrose, Tricia, 43–44
Push technology, 108–109

R

RealAudio, 32

Reno v. *ACLU*, 57
Rheingold, Howard, 35
Rimmer, Steve, 30–31

S

satellite Internet service, 106–107
search engines, 15–17,
scams, 44
Simon Wiesenthal Center, 49
Snyder, Joel, 100
Sorenson, Karen M., 52

T

telecommuting, 29–30
Teledesic Corporation, 106
Thomson, Malcolm, 26
trojan horse, 72

U

unlimited access plans, 94–95
urban myths, 41
U.S Department of Education, 28

V

van Wyk, Kenneth R., 72
Venditto, Gus, 47
videoconferencing, 97–98
viruses, 69–72
  hoaxes, 74, 75
  scanning software, 73

W

WebTV, 82–83
Weiner, Allan H., 16
Werner, Edward, 43
Winner, Langdon, 60
worms, 64–65, 72–73